No Common Thread

No Common Thread

The Selected Short Fiction of
Norma West Linder

First Edition

Hidden Brook Press
www.HiddenBrookPress.com
writers@HiddenBrookPress.com

Copyright © 2013 Hidden Brook Press
Copyright © 2013 Norma West Linder

All rights for story and characters revert to the author. All rights for book, layout and design remain with Hidden Brook Press. No part of this book may be reproduced except by a reviewer who may quote brief passages in a review. The use of any part of this publication reproduced, transmitted in any form or by any means, electronic, mechanical, photocopied, recorded or otherwise stored in a retrieval system without prior written consent of the publisher is an infringement of the copyright law.

This book is a work of fiction. Names, characters, places and events are either products of the author's imagination or are employed fictitiously. Any resemblance to actual events, locales or persons, living or dead, is entirely coincidental.

No Common Thread:
The Selected Short Fiction of Norma West Linder

Editor – James Deahl
Cover Design – Richard M. Grove
Layout and Design – Richard M. Grove

Typeset in Garamond
Printed and bound in USA

Library and Archives Canada Cataloguing in Publication

Linder, Norma West, 1928-
[Short stories. Selections]
    No common thread : the selected short fiction of Norma West Linder.

ISBN 978-1-897475-91-1 (pbk.)

    I. Title. II. Title: Selected short fiction of Norma West Linder.

PS8573.I53A6 2013   C813'.54   C2013-902875-7

For

JAMES EDWARD DEAHL

with love, always.

Acknowledgements

Most of these stories have been published in anthologies and periodicals. The author would like to thank the editors of the following publications for their support of her work.

Close to Quitting Time — The Love Letter
The Day Tripper — St. Nicholas Corrigan
Green's Magazine — The Poker Game, Seventh Day of May, This Mystery Person, and Ties that Bind
Horizon Magazine — Boxes, A City Slicker Goes Hunting, and Paddy and Pops
The Many Faces of Woman — Purple Heart
The Nashwaak Review — Bye Baby Bunting and Night of Wine and Roses
Niagara Branch CAA anthology — One Too Many
Origins — The Cornfield, Pumpkin Lady, and Sweet Comic Valentine
Pierian Spring — Saturation Point
Polished Pebbles – a Bluewater Anthology — The Night Visitor
River City Press Anthology — The Patchwork Comforter
Slice of Life — Meg Would Love to See You and Second Chance
Tales from the Manchester Arms — A Book by its Cover
Tale Spinners — Her Lucky Day and Two Grand Mothers
White Wall Review — Black Watch
Winner's Circle Anthology — Sam's Specialty

Contents

Foreword by Delia De Santis – *p. xiii*

– Purple Heart – *p. xvi*
– The Poker Game – *p. 6*
– This Mystery Person – *p. 12*
– Black Watch – *p. 22*
– A Good Turn – *p. 26*
– Sam's Specialty – *p. 30*
– Second Chance – *p. 38*
– Sweet Comic Valentine – *p. 42*
– Boxes – *p. 46*
– A Book By Its Cover – *p. 50*
– The Patchwork Comforter – *p. 56*
– Ice Cold Kindness – *p. 66*
– Saturation Point – *p. 70*
– Meg Would Love To See You – *p. 76*
– The Night Visitor – *p. 80*
– The Winter Of Netta Cooper's Discontent – *p. 86*
– Saint Nicholas Corrigan – *p. 96*
– Seventh Day Of May – *p. 100*
– More Time To Talk – *p. 108*
– The Love Letter – *p. 112*
– Two Grand Mothers – *p. 116*
– Ties That Bind – *p. 122*
– Paddy And Pops – *p. 128*
– The Cornfield – *p. 134*
– Night Of Wine And Roses – *p. 138*

— A City Slicker Goes Hunting — *p. 148*
— Madame Sylvia's Prediction — *p. 152*
— The Fishing Trip — *p. 158*
— Decision In Bangkok — *p. 162*
— One Too Many — *p. 170*
— Bye Baby Bunting — *p. 174*
— Her Lucky Day — *p. 180*
— Pumpkin Lady — *p. 184*

Afterword by Ryan Gibbs — *p. 191*
A Note on the Author — *p. 192*

Foreword

I first met Norma West Linder in the late 70s. A writing course was being offered at Lambton College in Sarnia, Ontario and she was going to be the instructor. I had read an article in the *Observer*, our local newspaper, about Ms. Linder having just joined the Writers' Union of Canada, at the time a young association of Canadian authors whose members included Margaret Laurence, Pierre Burton, Farley Mowatt, Margaret Atwood and other great names. Needless to say, it took a lot of courage for me an aspiring writer to sign up for the course with a well-known writer.

My fears were gone as soon as I saw Ms. Linder. The pretty young woman had a most pleasant demeanor, and immediately I felt relieved and glad I had decided to enroll in the course. I had read two of Ms. Linder's novels and my ambition was to someday be able to write just like her.

Ms. Linder was known as being one of our town's most prolific authors, with several published works to her credit. Included in these works were the hard cover novels *The Lemon Tree*, *Tangled Butterflies*, *Nahanni* (co-written with Hope Morritt), the mass market paperback *Woman in a Blue Hat*, and the memoir *Morels and Maple Syrup*. Not only was she our local writing icon, but she was also starting to get a much wider recognition.

From the 70s, fast-forward to the present, Ms. Linder has been steadily publishing all along. She is now the author of five novels, one book for children, one play, a memoir, fourteen poetry collections, one biography (co-authored with Hope Morritt), not to mention the dozens and dozens of short stories and articles she has published in newspapers, journals and literary reviews.

However, even with so much creative output to her credit, there was still one particular project she had not yet tackled: a book of short fiction. But knowing Norma West Linder's dedication to the written word, this too would soon be presented to her readers, her followers, and perhaps also to a brand new audience. We now have *No Common Thread: The Selected Short Fiction of Norma West Linder*.

Ms. Linder has chosen a memorable title for this thought provoking and entertaining gathering of stories. Upon hearing the title, I was pleased that this book didn't follow the somewhat traditional, and perhaps overdone, format where a so called collection is made up of connected stories. In *No Common Thread* the stories do not follow the life of one character in different situations, nor that of different characters linked to one another by relationship or by genealogy. Each story follows different people altogether, during a particular time of conflict in their lives. We come across a great variety of characters, carefully gleaned out of a broad spectrum of humanity, giving the reader an all inclusive view of our world as Ms. Linder perceives it.

But upon further reflection, I also found the title, *No Common Thread*, to be a carefully chosen oxymoron that signifies a deeper meaning of what one has read. There is a thematic "coming together" in the multilayered stories that is not blatantly obvious, but to be pleasantly discovered. This profound linkage derives from the author's notable regard for *goodness*: her strong empathy for people impoverished in various ways, and by her sensibility in understanding the strong need for human beings to retain their pride. Ms. Linder deals with the "strong" with grace and the "weak" with understanding and consideration. And, at times, she is not afraid to pitch us right into the world of the disadvantaged and the less privileged, and even the undesirables.

All in all, the fictional world of Ms. Linder is populated with people from all walks of life; we have a great aunt, a lesbian mother, a ten-year-old tomboy, a neighbour, a widow, an alcoholic, a super clean mom, a honeymooning couple, a homicide officer, a penniless student, a keynote speaker at a Newcomers' club, and many more ordinary and not so ordinary characters whose lives are laid bare in front of us in the thirty-three stories in the book.

Not to be ignored is the fact that we are often made to ponder at people's misfortunes, and sometimes even made to chuckle at the extent of people's silliness. And more importantly, we are brought to *look at* and examine our own actions toward others and toward ourselves.

Ms. Linder is also a believer of second chances in life. In "Ties That Bind," a mother faced with the loss of her son unexpectedly leaving home, is jolted out of the grief she had been trapped in since a plane crash had taken her daughter's life. So, when the son makes a collect call home, she accepts the "charge" with unabashed joy. "Come home, Kevie, we need you." With such simple words, the author makes us feel that deep warmth felt by a mother who is going to be reunited with her son.

The author also approaches the complexity of the human mind with great insight. For example, Peter, in the very short but compelling story, "The Cornfield," says: "Once I cut both my wrists. They said the blood was terrible. I didn't want to die, though. I just wanted to kill myself. It's not the same thing." In this story, the author does not give us answers for the mind-pain felt by Peter, nor does she try to explain the obscure meaning of his cry for help. But she does better, she lays it all in front of us, open wounds and all, and let's us "see" and "feel," for ourselves.

A couple of the shorter pieces in the book are real gems, such as the flirtatious and fun "Meg Would Love to See You" and the very suspenseful "A Good Turn." And several of the stories I would enjoy reading over and over again. Among them, I would choose, "The Winter of Netta Cooper's Discontent", "Purple Heart", and "Pumpkin Lady."

Throughout the book, I couldn't help but admire Ms. Linder's ear for dialogue. There is nothing unnatural in the way her people talk. She keeps them in character so well that they become real people in one's mind. They can be an old lady, a teenager, a loverboy, a policeman, whatever one happens to be on the stage of life, and she knows their lingo.

Norma West Linder has put together an admirable collection of short fiction. She has given us tragedy, humour, mystery and even magic. Even though she has varied ways to tell a story, she never strays away from her own distinct voice.

Well-known poet James Deahl, in his Editor's introduction to Norma West Linder's latest book of poetry titled *Adder's-tongues*, states: "Her writing has grace and simplicity." To that I would like to add that such enduring qualities and ideals have no boundaries, rendering appeal for Ms. Linder's work universal.

Delia De Santis,
author of,
Fast Forward and Other Stories

Purple Heart

Beth Burkhart woke early, Grant's deep, remembered voice disturbing her sleep. "You deserve a medal for sticking with me all these years, old girl. You should get a Purple Heart."

"That's an American medal, isn't it?"

"Good for you. You know your medals."

"I haven't been married to a history buff all these years without learning something," she'd replied, wondering just when he had begun calling her old girl. Now she would give anything just to hear him use those words again.

The Purple Heart had become a standing joke between them — a joke not shared by their two sons and daughter, Erica. Beth knew only too well the boys had never really forgiven their father, the Chief, for being so hard on them when they were young. Not that he'd ever actually been unfair. Grant was a just man. Always had been. But teenagers were not like police recruits. You couldn't just bark orders and expect them to be implicitly obeyed. Life wasn't that simple. Still in all, she reflected as she turned her damp pillow over, the three Burkhart offspring had survived adolescence to become reasonably well-adjusted adults. The boys — even though they were grown men, she and Erica still called them "the boys" — were now partners in a successful computer business of their own in Regina. Erica was teaching high school French up in North Bay, and, for the most part, found her work rewarding. Now married and the mother of two active youngsters, Erica was beginning to understand her father the Chief a lot better.

"I catch myself yelling at Jimmy or Judy and I sound just like him," she confessed. "Eddie teases me about it."

Last night Beth had returned from a hectic two-week visit with Erica and her family. She'd arrived home late and gone straight to bed without unpacking first — or even brushing her teeth.

* * *

"You wouldn't have approved of that, would you, Grant?" Beth directed the question at her bedroom ceiling from the big brass bed that seemed too large, too cold, and too empty without her husband's solid presence. They had been inordinately proud of their renovated master bedroom with its en suite bath and Jacuzzi. Best of all was an inviting little balcony outside a pair of sliding French doors. With their family grown and gone, she and Grant had often taken their morning coffee out there, quietly enjoying the view of the tree-lined street below, lost in separate worlds yet finding comfort in each other's company. A far cry from the chaotic days of packing school lunches in the mornings.

The April sun was slanting into the bedroom now, lighting in turn her various treasures — the water-colour of lilacs Erica had done in Grade Twelve, the copper scrap sculpture of jazz musicians the boys had created together, the crystal vase Grant had given her for their thirty-fifth wedding anniversary. He'd taken to gardening in earnest after his retirement from the force and the vase had always been filled with whatever flowers were in season: forsythia, lilacs, tulips, roses, and zinnias. The vase was empty now, like Grant's side of the bed.

Everybody said the first year was the worst. Drumming her fingers on the blue chenille bedspread, Beth counted the months since mid-November. Well, she'd endured half the worst.

Spasms of pain continued to catch her unaware at odd times. She wondered how long that would go on. The sharp grief of seeing his handwriting, of finding his old reading glasses under a sofa cushion …

He'd adored Erica until she'd changed from a compliant little girl to a rebellious teenager. Beth always tried to be the buffer between them. "You're too lenient," he'd shout. "You'll spoil her. You mark my words."

He'd frequently threatened to take his belt to their daughter but hadn't actually done so. The closest he came was when he caught her sneaking a bottle of rye out of the liquor cabinet when she was fifteen. He'd grounded her for two weeks. "Beat me, Dad," she had cried. "Please, beat me. Don't ground me!"

* * *

Beth smiled, remembering. She'd felt like smacking Erica herself the time she'd taken Beth's best Hudson Bay blanket and cut a hole in it to make a poncho for a beach party. She and Erica had enjoyed a good laugh recalling that incident over a festive Easter dinner, the grandchildren revelling in tales of their mother's wrongdoing.

Christmas had been bad for her, for all of them. She'd spent the holiday season in Regina with the boys and their current girlfriends. Sometimes she wondered if either of her sons would ever settle down. Skirt chasers, they'd have been called in the old days. They seemed happy, though, and they'd made a point, for her sake, of trying to recall their father's good qualities. How he'd always stressed the value of education, of hard work paying off in the end, just so long as it was work a man liked. That's why he was successful in his work, he'd explained. He'd made it to Police Chief because he liked what he did.

Grant should never have taken his belt to the boys, Beth thought. But at least he'd never done so in a temper. Looking back, it seemed to her the worst fights they had were always over how to raise their children. Perhaps she had been too easy on them. The boys had been more than a handful in their early teens. It must have embarrassed Grant at times. She didn't even try to stop him from punishing them when, at fourteen and sixteen, they'd stolen a school bus and driven it all the way from Sarnia to Petrolia.

She should get up, Beth told herself. Keeping busy was supposed to be the best medicine. Maybe she should think about going back to her part-time job in the bookstore. It might take her mind off everything for a few hours a week.

* * *

How brave Grant had been throughout his illness! Far braver than she could have been. Pancreatic cancer. A nightmare. Yet last fall he'd driven to his favourite nursery and come home with more bulbs than she'd ever seen him buy before. All through September, he was out in the front yard planting them, preparing for a spring he knew he would never see.

She hated gardening herself. The first June bug carcass she unearthed put an end to any attempt to share her husband's passion for digging in the soil. Her passion was writing poetry. Grant considered that hobby a deviation from the norm. He couldn't understand why she was so thrilled to have little publications accept her work. "You don't even get paid," he'd say.

"I get free copies," she'd explain. "I like reading the work of other poets."

She smiled now, recalling how it had taken years for her to work up the courage to call herself a poet. No, she and Grant hadn't had much in common. For her, it had been a strong physical attraction in the beginning. He'd surprised her by returning her ardour tenfold when they were alone together. In public, though, he wouldn't tolerate any show of affection. He'd come from a British background where hugging was an alien activity. Even in front of the kids, he was reticent. She'd occasionally tried giving him a daytime hug, but there was always a certain rigidity in him and she finally quit trying. But their sex life continued to be satisfying, sometimes even surprisingly exciting. Right up until that awful visit to the clinic …

Now the sun was spotlighting the framed photo of Grant in his uniform on the wall across from her. Police Chief Grant Burkhart. She reached for her glasses on the end table and put them on to see his face more clearly. A handsome man with well-chiselled features and piercing blue eyes. "Why couldn't you unbend a little?" she asked aloud. "Why didn't you tell me you loved me over ham and eggs instead of only whispering it when we were alone in bed? Why?"

* * *

Nature was calling. When the call could no longer be denied, Beth slipped out of bed and plodded barefoot across the room. She caught sight of herself in the full-length double mirrors of the clothes closet. A fat dumpling of a woman under a cloud of white hair. Hard to believe she'd once been good-looking enough to turn heads. A wealth of dark curls framing an oval face. Chocolate brown eyes. A generous smile. She and Grant had met when they were both twenty, shortly after she'd learned to drive. He had stopped her for a minor traffic infraction, and she'd joked that he'd given her orders ever since.

Their grandchildren had inherited her brown eyes. Strict as he'd been with Erica and the boys, Jimmy and Judy could do no wrong as far as Grant was concerned. How he had doted on them!

Beth brushed her teeth and smiled at her mirrored image. She hadn't really looked attractive for years. No wonder Grant had been so stingy with compliments. His most flattering remark to her had been that she deserved a medal — a Purple Heart — for putting up with him. Not much to hold onto. Well, he'd never been a demonstrative man. That was that.

She splashed cold water over her face, combed her hair, pulled on a pink terrycloth robe with matching slippers and made her way to the sliding French doors of the balcony. Grant's last words were echoing around her. "Keep your chin up, old girl. Do it for me." This from his hospital bed, his face whiter than his pillow.

She had promised him she would be stoic, and she had tried. But her attempts had been futile. She'd cried shamelessly at the funeral, howled like a banshee in front of the boys during the Christmas holidays, clung sobbing to Erica just last week. Once, she'd broken down in the food court in the nearby mall, losing control before dozens of curious strangers. All because she'd seen a young father carrying his little daughter atop his shoulders, exactly the way Grant had carried Erica. A long time ago. A lifetime ago.

* * *

Beth opened the doors and stepped out into the sunshine of the early April morning. As she looked down, her eyes widened in disbelief. There, on the square of lawn below, bloomed a huge purple heart — a heart shaped of crocuses in glorious colour. In its centre, her initial B, in yellow crocuses, stood out clearly against the tender green grass. Tears came again, but this time they were gentle, healing ones. She made no attempt to wipe them away.

The Poker Game

It was snowing the day they threw The Cowboy out. I wasn't surprised to see him sitting there. I'd seen it coming for a long time. Most of the tenants thought he got exactly what he deserved. Still, I don't know — it was sort of sad the way the snow was piling up on his meager belongings. Big, soft flakes covering all that shabbiness. It made me feel sorry for him in spite of his bad reputation.

His worldly goods consisted of a ratty looking single bed, a couple of caved-in suitcases, a few pots and pans (half filled with snow), a hot plate, and a wooden kitchen suite that was obviously on its last legs. The only thing holding the table together was a thick coating of chipped yellow paint. Somebody had once put decals on the back of the chairs. Roses. Big, red roses.

The Cowboy was sitting on one of those chairs when Grace Simmons and I left for the mall around four o'clock Friday afternoon. None of us knew his real name. We called him The Cowboy because he always wore a wide-brimmed black hat, blue jeans, and a black leather jacket over a matching silk shirt that strained hard against his beer belly. Both his body and his clothes looked perpetually unwashed. His scraggly dark hair framed a pale, bony face. When he smiled, which rarely happened, his teeth looked like tiny broken tombstones. He didn't have much going for him in the way of looks. Or anything else, for that matter. Still, I don't know ... there was something about him. Maybe it was the old-fashioned way he tipped his hat to me whenever we passed each other.

I suppose it was his drinking that finally did it. But I didn't sign the petition to have him put out. There are worse characters than him in our building. There's big Harry on the first floor. His own wife's afraid to say boo to him. Ever since Jersey Gardens was taken over by the Ontario Housing Corporation we've harbored all sorts of so-called undesirables. This place used to be a quiet-to-the-point-of-dull apartment building for seniors only. Now it's full of people of all ages. People with problems. People who *are* problems.

I once caught The Cowboy looking for cigarette butts in the foyer, and I offered him ten bucks to move my living room furniture around. Told him I was sick of things looking the same all the time. That was the truth, too. But The Cowboy had his pride. "I don't take no charity," he'd growled.

He did move my sofa though. For free. Unfortunately, he had some grease on his hands at the time, and the stains never did come out of the gold velour.

When Grace and I got back from the mall at six-thirty, The Cowboy was still perched on his kitchen chair. He looked as though he hadn't budged an inch. It was growing dark, and it was still snowing. I could picture him sitting there all night, turning into a huge frozen snowman wearing a sparkling white cowboy hat. He didn't even look up when Grace and I went by, picking our way carefully so we wouldn't slip on a treacherous patch of ice.

"Do you suppose he let something boil over on the stove again?" I asked, as we stood in the warm hallway waiting for the elevator. "I thought I heard the fire engines late the other night."

I hadn't even bothered to get out of bed when I heard the sirens. Having firemen come to Jersey Gardens was getting to be a regular occurrence. A month or so ago I was out in the hallway when they came and wanting to help I asked one of them if he knew the way to the laundry room where the fire was supposed to have started. "Lady," he'd replied, "I could find my way blindfolded around this building."

The elevator was even slower than usual in coming. It gave me time to think. Too much time, maybe. I started remembering stories we'd heard about how The Cowboy's father used to abuse him when he was just a little kid.

"Grace, he'll freeze out there," I said. "He probably hasn't a cent in his pockets. I'm going to ask him in. He can spend the night in my apartment."

"Rita Jennings, you're crazy!" she exclaimed. "You'll be murdered in your bed. Or worse."

I couldn't help laughing. "Grace, what could be worse?"

"You know perfectly well what I mean." She drew her lips into a thin little line. I looked at her upswept grey hair, her pale skin, and her faded blue eyes behind their pearly frames. It was almost like looking at a mirror.

"We're old ladies, Grace. We can't be sexy, but we can be kind."

"You can't be serious. Rita Jennings, if I didn't know you better I'd think you were on dope like half the newcomers in here."

"Did you sign the petition to have him evicted, Grace?"

"I most certainly did. We don't need trash like him. I signed it, and I got plenty of others to sign it too."

Leaving her standing there, I made my way back through the foyer and out to the boulevard fronting our building.

"You can't stay out here," I told The Cowboy. "Come up and spend the night in my apartment. My sofa, the one you moved for me, pulls out into a bed. It's very comfortable. In the morning, you can figure out what to do."

"Hell with it," he muttered. "Hell with all of them. I'm staying put." In the glow of the street light, his brown eyes looked wild.

"You can't sit here all night. Come along. I'll make you some tea. And I've got some good beef stew I can warm up."

"I don't need no charity."

"It won't be charity. I washed my curtains, and I can't put them back up by myself. You can help me." But I'll see to it you wash your hands first, I thought. "Come on," I urged. "It's getting cold out here."

He looked around to see if anyone was watching, but there wasn't a soul about. Huge flakes of snow were falling softly all around. They looked feathery and beautiful in the golden glow of the street lights. Finally, he got to his feet, brushed away the snow, took off his hat and shook it vigorously. "I guess I can hang them curtains for you," he said. "I'll just leave my stuff here. It ain't worth doodly squat anyways."

He strode ahead to the door and waited for me to open it with my key.

I knew the story would be all over the building within twenty-four hours. Grace would see to that. Telling gossip is the only thing she enjoys more than listening to it. Sometimes I think the only grace she has is in her name. After all, maybe The Cowboy is a born loser but ...

Born loser. The words gave me an idea. "Do you know how to play poker?" I asked as we entered my apartment.

"Sure do," he said. "Been playing it most of my life. My old lady showed me how when I was eleven. Just before she took off for parts unknown."

"Do you play for money?"

"What else?"

"Would you teach me? I'd love to try my hand at gambling."

"Sure. I guess so."

"Good. And don't worry if we play for high stakes. I can afford it. What's your real name?"

He looked suspicious. "Waddya mean, my real name?"

"I mean, well, I'm afraid I don't know your name."

"It's Hal. Hal Vincent."

"How do you do, Mr. Vincent."

"Hal's good enough. Now where's them curtains?"

"First things first." Smiling, I shoved a towel into his hands and pointed him towards the bathroom. "Wash up and we'll eat."

We started in playing cards as soon as my gold drapes were back in place over the sliding balcony doors. Nobody could spy on us.

I knew how to play poker. My grandfather had taught me when I was a girl. But I'm a pretty fair actress when I want to be. I didn't spend five years with the local little theatre group for nothing. I made my bad luck look real. Maybe he'll blow it all on booze, I thought. Or maybe he won't. He might just join that girlfriend he told me about on the West Coast. In any case, I have more money than I'm ever likely to need. And nobody in this wide world to leave it to.

Early the next morning, Hal Vincent left, walking on air in his old down-at-the-heels cowboy boots. He was more than eight hundred dollars richer. His cheeks bloomed with color — just like the roses on his discarded kitchen chairs. And he hadn't taken "no charity".

ns Person
This Mystery Person

When Beth entered the kitchen, her brother Harold was finishing off the last of her homemade strawberry jam.

"What are you doing up so early?" she asked, reaching for the coffee filters.

"Couldn't sleep," he muttered between huge bites of toast. "Didn't sleep a wink all night."

"Thinking about Cheryl?" Her voice, Beth noted, had taken on that solicitous tone she was trying to erase.

"Nope. It's that bed of Jackson's. How he can sleep on such a hard mattress is beyond me."

Beth felt a stab of annoyance. Harold had been staying with them for three weeks now, and was no nearer to a solution to his marital problems than he'd been when he'd prevailed upon her to take him in. The apartment was too small for the four of them, but he'd been able to get around her — as usual. She'd always felt maternal about Harold. Though he'd turned twenty-nine, he seemed closer in age to Jackson, their seventeen-year-old son, whose room he was occupying. But he couldn't go on staying with them indefinitely. She'd tell him tonight, she vowed. He'd have to make other arrangements.

Jackson came stumbling into the kitchen, curly blonde hair tousled, blue eyes still misty with sleep. "What's the time, Mom?" he asked, yawning prodigiously.

"Clock's right," she replied.

He glanced up at the ceramic clock on the wall above her head. "Twenty-five to eight! Jeez, Mom, why didn't you call me? You knew I had to get up early for band practice."

"I gave you the alarm clock."

"I didn't hear it. Jeez, I still have to wash my hair."

"Looks clean to me," she offered.

"Clean! It's so full of oil I should be declared a national asset."

"Well, if you're late now, Jackson …"

"I'll just have to be good and late. I've gotta wash it. We're not having

Greaser Day at school." He began dumping Cheerios into a bowl. "I'm not skipping breakfast, either. You should've called me."

Beth was about to warn him he'd taken too much cereal for the size of the bowl when he tipped the milk pitcher over it. The liquid spread rapidly over the table.

"Jackson!" she shouted. "My ten-year olds are more careful than you." She grabbed a terrycloth tea towel and began swiping at the mess as Harold jumped to his feet, brushing milk from his brown corduroy jeans. "I have to wear these today!" he roared, "unless your mother's planning to do the washing before she goes to school."

"Well I'm not!" she snapped. "What do you think I am? Superwoman? I have to get ready yet myself."

"What in hell's going on in here?"

The kitchen trio turned towards the open doorway. Beth was only too aware of the ludicrous picture they made in contrast with her meticulously groomed husband. "I'll have breakfast downtown," Jack announced, his handsome face disdainful. The sooner I get out of this madhouse, the better. Beth, where's my briefcase?"

"In the front hall. Right where you left it." Attempting a lighter tone, she added, "Better take your umbrella. Looks like an April shower day."

Jackson was calmly eating as though he had all the time in the world. Great, she thought. Another late slip. Third one this month. The boy wasn't getting his proper rest on the living room sofa. Harold simply had to clear out. Life was too hectic. Somebody always wanting to get into the bathroom. And the cooking and cleaning! There should be signs on the kitchen and laundry room: WE NEVER CLOSE. No, it was too much. It couldn't go on. Jack was becoming irritable; he wasn't the easiest natured man in the world to begin with. Times like this she had to keep reminding herself of his good qualities. Thrift, fidelity, and intelligence. Sounded deadly dull. Seeing him in the doorway just now she'd had a mad desire to run her milky fingers through his just-so hair and down over his pin-striped navy suit.

But Harold would have to go. Even she, with all her patience, had come to the end of her rope. She wasn't about to tie a knot in it and hold on.

Jackson pushed back his chair. "Mom, we're having a vocab test on *Brave New World* this aft. Would you jot down a few definitions for me?"

"Aren't you supposed to look them up in your dictionary?"

"Can't find it. Anyway, you're faster." He gave her his most appealing look. "Please, Mom. I can't afford to fail this test. My book's on the dining room table."

"You can't afford any more late slips either," she retorted, but he was already on his way to the shower.

"Beth, would you pour me another coffee?" Harold asked, glancing up from his *Toronto Life* magazine. "It's really good this morning. You must have added a dash of salt like I suggested."

She hadn't, but she didn't say so. She did, however, pour the coffee. It would be the last one, she told herself. He had to go. She'd tell him at noon, when they could talk privately. By the time Jack got home it would be settled. He'd be no help in any case. He seemed to enjoy having another man around. "At least I can talk sports and politics with him," he'd told her. "He's not like your usual little theatre twerp."

But her mind was made up. Harold could give up his theatrical ideas and go back to Cheryl in Sarnia, or he could stay in the city and move into the Y. Where he went wasn't her concern. As long as he went. "Will you be here at noon?" she asked.

"Far as I know. Why?"

"Nothing. We'll talk then." She headed for the dining room.

"If Victor calls, I'll be gone," he shouted after her. "I can act, dammit. I'm bound to get a break soon."

You're acting all the time, she silently accused him. You might as well get paid for it. The thought made her feel mean-spirited. She recalled how good Harold had been in little theatre roles in their hometown. Good enough to turn professional. Everyone had said so. And finally, Harold had listened to them.

She couldn't blame him, really. He'd been outstanding in that last production. She'd forgotten it was her brother up on that stage when he'd played that part in *Look Homeward Angel*. It was too bad, though, about Cheryl. When he'd married her three years ago he'd shared her dream of a home and family. Beth knew she'd been banking part of her receptionist's pay along with her hopes for that future. She liked Cheryl. And she felt sorry for her. No death is without pain, she reflected. And the death of a dream is particularly painful.

But Harold's dream had changed. All he wanted now was to land the role of Jake the bartender in *After Ours*. He'd read for it a week ago and was spending desperate hours by the phone, his tension almost palpable.

Beth picked up her son's notebook. Good thing she was only a block away from her school, she thought. She was invariably the last one out in the morning.

Jackson's most recent vocabulary test floated out and landed on the floor. She picked it up and saw that he'd made only eighteen out of a possible fifty. When she began to read it, she couldn't help smiling. The words *were* difficult — especially when taken out of context.

She was just finishing his homework when Jackson hurried in, his blonde hair a tribute to the marvels of shampoo, cream rinse, and blow drier. She waved the test under his nose. "What's the meaning of this!" she demanded.

"Please, mother mine, no more definitions."

"We are not amused."

"Mizz Hocksteader wasn't amused either. That's why she failed me. Anyway, how am I supposed to remember that *fitchews* and *cockchafers* are polecats and beetles?"

"That's no excuse for calling the first bubblegum for spastics. I won't even repeat what you put for the second."

"You're blushing, Mom."

"I am not. For corporeal mass you put a guy's weight in the army. Really, Jackson!"

"Well you told me never to leave any blanks. Always try, you said. So I tried."

She gave up. "Don't forget your lunch money. It's on the kitchen table."

Beth's morning passed quickly. Her class, consisting of thirteen boys and seven girls was larger than last year's. Outnumbered by males here as well as on the home front, she mused. But she enjoyed working with the Grade Fivers. Ten was a marvelous age. Her students were still curious, still open to life. They liked a challenge. Instead of a collective groan, she'd received a burst of enthusiasm from them last week when she'd assigned them to write a composition on a "Mystery Person" of their choice. The pieces were due this afternoon. They were looking forward to reading them aloud and having the class name the person they were describing. No doubt most of them would be easy-to-guess TV personalities.

When Beth arrived home at noon she found her brother hunched over a drink at the dining room table. "You look like one of Jake the bartender's best customers," she teased.

"Funny you should say that. I just got the news that Victor doesn't want me for that role in *After Ours*. Nor for any other role either."

"Oh, Harold, I'm sorry."

"You're sorry. I'm sorry. We're all sorry." He looked up at her, his blue eyes bitter with pain. He reminded her so much of Jackson as a little boy she instinctively reached down and patted his head.

He took a large gulp of his drink. "Rye and marriage, on the rocks," he muttered. "Beth, do you think I should try dying my hair black? Maybe I don't look dramatic enough. God, I wish I had Jack's looks. Maybe I should grow a mustache, or a beard. Only a blonde beard isn't any good …"

Beth left him to his ruminations and went into the kitchen. "Would you like a grilled cheese sandwich?" she called out after a few minutes.

"How can you talk about food at a time like this!" he roared.

Poor Harold. How could she tell him now? As she picked up the chrome kettle, she caught her face in its reflection. A wavering pink blob.

Over her mug of instant coffee she decided to wait till after school and tell him then, when he'd had a little time to recover from his disappointment about the play.

* * *

The English compositions were so thoroughly involving Beth forgot her problems and joined her students in guessing identities. As she'd anticipated, most of them were about rock or film stars. One, however, was different from the others. It was read by Ritchie Cameron, a boy who'd given her a good deal of trouble back in September. He glanced nervously around the room and cleared his throat twice before he started. "This Mystery Person is not very big but she's got a big voice and everybody listens to her. She's taller than me and her hair is sort of yellow. She wears lots of make-up and nice clothes. Sometimes she takes me to fire stations and places like that, and once I got lost in a museum. She tells me interesting things — like how it takes a whole lot of maple sap to make a little bit of maple syrup. She says life's like that — that it takes a whole lot of living to get a little bit smart. She's mean sometimes, but mostly she's a neat person."

The moment he finished reading, every arm in the room shot up.

"It's our teacher!" cried the first girl Ritchie called upon.

Beth was filled with quiet pleasure. The giftie had just given her the power to see herself as her students saw her.

She was still nursing that joy at four-thirty when she'd finished marking the compositions and preparing work for the next day. She'd been tempted to give

Ritchie an A, but because of the number of mistakes he'd made, she penned only the deserved B. She tucked the composition into her purse to re-read later.

Harold met her at the apartment door, his cheeks flushed, speech slurring as he asked, "Could you lend me twenty, Beth?"

"What do you want it for?"

"What?"

"A reasonable question, Harold. What for?"

"Wanna go downtown for a coupla drinks."

"You don't need any more. You need something to eat. I have a pot roast ready to heat up for dinner."

"Please, Sis?"

"Absolutely not."

She turned away from the very surprised and slightly bloodshot blue eyes. She couldn't remember ever having refused him anything before. But she was right. He'd had more than enough to drink. It wasn't like him to overdo it this way. "Is Jackson home from school?" she asked, trying to make casual conversation.

"He's in my … his room."

The pronominal reference did not go unnoticed. As soon as he sobers up, she told herself. He needs to grow up. Cheryl's the one who's trying …

A blast of hard rock precluded further ruminations. Jackson had better turn that music down before his father got home. No man's home was his castle these days — not if it contained a seventeen-year-old rock fan.

As evidence of the latest phase he was going through, Jackson's door was locked. She had to pound several times before he heard her and opened it. "Okay, Mom. I'll put on my headphones."

"Do that. How you can concentrate on homework with all that noise is beyond me."

"Listen to this part on drums. It's awesome!" He slipped the headphones over her ears just as Jack came to the door, looking as impeccable as he had in the morning — and almost as angry. She read his lips as he turned to their son. "Unplug your mother. I want to talk to her."

"Talk away," she offered when Jackson relieved her of the headset.

"I can't find my track suit. Did the laundry get done?"

"What do you mean 'get done'? You say that as though the laundry gets up on long gray legs and totters down to the basement to do itself."

"Good Lord! I just asked a simple question."

"Well next time don't use the passive voice of the verb. Just come right out and ask, Did you do the laundry?"

She saw him wink at Jackson and found it hard to control her irritation.

"What do you need washed?"

"My track suit. Going to run a few blocks with Harold."

Might do her brother good at that, she thought. Help sober him up. And they'd both be out of the way while she got dinner ready. "Your suit's clean," she said. "It's in your bottom drawer. Maybe you can manage to find it all by yourself."

Could she be going through some sort of mid-life crisis? Beth asked herself as she began to peel carrots. Little things seemed to bother her lately. It wasn't like her to be so sarcastic. She'd always taken care of the laundry without complaint. And she didn't have to make strawberry jam. She could just buy a jar instead. Maybe thirty-nine was a difficult age. Could facing forty be getting to her?

But maybe it wasn't her age at all. Maybe the unfairness of the workload was becoming insupportable. She'd once read a news item in which a police commissioner had referred to women as "balls of fluff in the eyes of the Creator". The ridiculous words had stayed with her as though engraved somewhere in her consciousness. She thought of her best friend — raising five kids all by herself. Balls of fluff? Balls! She chuckled as she tossed the last carrot into the pressure cooker.

After dinner, Beth gave in to the urge to read Ritchie Cameron's composition to her family. "Guess who the Mystery Person is," she challenged.

Jack glanced up from the Sports section of his newspaper. "Sounds like that girl from Sesame Street."

Jackson shook his head. "I think it's the chick on that Saturday morning kids' show."

Harold didn't bother guessing until she prompted him. "Is it the boy's mother?"

"I can't believe this!" Beth jumped up and surveyed the three of them. "Don't any of you see me in that description? No, Jack. Don't do that. Don't you dare put on that maybe-it's-that-time of the month look." She waved the paper above her head like a flag. "This is an English composition about *me*. It's time for some changes around here — starting now."

Jackson broke the silence that followed. "Speaking of English comp, Mom, could you give me a hand with …"

"I'll give you a hand, all right. I'll give you a great big hand — the moment you prove you're actually capable of doing your assignments all by yourself."

For once, her son failed to make a joking reply.

She turned to her husband. "Jack, tomorrow I'm going to give you a ten-minute crash course in the operation of a washer and drier. Should be a snap for a civil engineer. It's either that or do without a clean track suit when you want one."

Harold spoke up. "Any coffee left, Beth? My head feels like it's coming apart at the seams."

She was about to tell him to go make his own coffee but decided it would be a good time to tell him to clear out instead. Still, she didn't want to embarrass him in front of the others. "Come out to the kitchen, Harold, and I'll make you a mug of instant."

She waited till he had his first sip before she began. She was no longer hesitant about broaching the subject. She wasn't doing her kid brother any favours by letting him stay on and on. Besides, he wasn't a kid anymore. She sat down across the table from him. "We have to talk, Harold. It's been quite a while since …"

"I'll save you the trouble, Sis. I know what you're going to say. I'm leaving tomorrow." He attempted a smile that didn't quite come off. "You know the expression — after three days house guests and fish start to stink. I've been here three weeks."

"I'm sorry, Harold. I wish you *had* landed the role of Jake the bartender. You're a good actor. You'd have done a good job."

He looked at her, blue eyes shining. "Maybe it's better I didn't get the part. I'm not so sure it's the life for me. Being in community productions is fun. But depending on the theatre for a living is something else. Anyway, I miss Cheryl. More that I can say. Right now I can't see a better life than the traditional house with a mortgage and a couple of kids."

Beth smiled. "Go and call her. You can use the phone in our bedroom. You'll have privacy there."

After he left, Beth remained at the kitchen table, elbows resting on the woven red place mat in front of her, chin cupped in her hands. She felt a pleasant fatigue. It had been quite a day.

Black Watch

If I don't go, I'll feel guilty. So it's up the short concrete walk and in through the double set of glass doors. One of the caregivers hurries forward to lock the last door behind me. Visiting a prison must be something like this.

I find her in the cafeteria, sitting at a small table with another patient, a middle-aged bald man I've never seen before. He's wearing a gray and maroon striped bathrobe. A slot in the wooden panel on the wall above our heads informs us today is Tuesday, April 24th, 1989. I try to make conversation about the spring weather being unseasonably warm, but it's no go. They simply look from their coffee mugs to me and back again. At last the man gets up and shuffles off, leaving us alone near the door to her private room.

I hand her the usual box of Laura Secord chocolates. What else can I give her? She's still able to enjoy treats. Like a child, she rips off the ribbon, tears away the fancy gold paper, opens the box. Then she just looks at it as though she's forgotten what to do next. Slowly, she replaces the lid and sets the chocolates on the white plastic table between us.

She's wearing a navy woolen skirt with a matching long-sleeved sweater — along with every piece of jewelry she owns. Rings, gold and silver chains, bracelets, brooches, earrings, a watch, the lot. She's afraid of having her belongings stolen.

"That's a pretty ring," I say, trying to keep the silences filled. "That pearl one."

All the wrinkles on her face move upwards in a smile. She's almost girlish. "Do you like it? Really?"

I make the ring conversation last as long as possible. She's no longer with me when I try to move on to other pieces of jewelry. Suddenly, she tells me I haven't changed a bit since we all lived in Toronto. That's more than forty years ago.

I return the pleasant falsehood, thinking all the while of the way she used to be. Like a Dresden doll. Blonde and delicate with china blue eyes. The eyes are mirrors of the soul. Her eyes are no longer mirrors. The light has gone out of them. They reflect nothing.

"I think I'll move back to Canada," she says.

It's well over a year since she left Mississippi, but she thinks she's still in the States. I don't want to upset her, so I agree that such a move might be a good idea. I turn the conversation back to food and fashions — safe topics. But now my mind is wandering.

She's the only one left. Her two brothers have passed away — both from heart attacks. One of them was my husband. For some reason, I find myself recalling a picnic we had when we were living on Centre Island in 1948. People could live on the Island then. My late husband and I worked in Toronto, but we both loved the beach so one summer we rented what we could afford there — a large, glassed-in front porch on Mohawk Street. Not roomy, but sufficient for our needs at the time. I remember how my sister-in-law came over on the ferry with her three children and my mother-in-law. The beach was the only place big enough for us all to be together. In a black and white snapshot in one of my old albums, my sister-in-law and I have our faces pressed cheek to cheek, smiling through the open circle of an inner tube. In that picture, she doesn't look eighteen years my senior. We look like a couple of Hollywood starlets. It seems like a lifetime ago. It *is* a lifetime ago. I've been studying those old pictures a lot lately. Searching for answers.

I glance at my watch. And hour's visit is long enough. But she wants me to go with her to her room. I leave the door ajar, but she pulls it shut. Low music is coming form the television set in the corner by the window. Community messages flash across the bright blue screen.

"Why don't you change the channel?" I ask. "Sometimes there are good shows on in the afternoon."

"I can't understand them," she replies. "Can't follow them. Can't remember what they're saying."

Her daughters have covered the pale yellow walls of her room with pictures of relatives — relatives she remembers only fleetingly. Three large dolls take up most of her narrow bed. One is a fat pink baby doll clad in a long white flannelette gown. One is a lady doll in a pink satin formal. The third is a Scottish lassie with thick chestnut curls. She's dressed in black velvet and tartan. I recognize the tartan. It's called Black Watch.

"They keep taking them out of my bed," my sister-in-law complains. "But I always put them back."

"There's hardly room for you," I protest. "Let's put them up on that shelf. They'd look good up there."

She moves closer to me. "Do you know why I keep them in my bed?" she asks, her voice lowered to a tone of conspiracy.

I shake my head. The silence becomes oppressive.

She goes on in a whisper. "I keep them there because I don't want to die alone."

The three dolls seem to be staring straight at me. I have to go. We hug. I try, as always, to talk her into staying in her room. But she follows me every step of the way back to the front doors of the building. After several more hugs, one of the caregivers comes to my rescue. I promise to return soon, knowing in my heart I'll put it off as long as possible.

Retracing my steps along the front walk, I look back only once. She's staring out through the clear glass doors, her round face like a full white moon.

The April sun is unusually strong. There's a light breeze stirring red and yellow tulips and the grass on either side of me is emerald green. I still feel that same odd sense of guilt. I can't get the image of those dolls out of my head. Those reaching arms. Arms that seem to implore …

At home, I take my newspaper from the mailbox, make myself a strong cup of tea, and sit down to try to immerse myself in the world news. But an item of local interest is first to catch my eye. It's about the nursing home I've just visited. The owners are closing it because of financial difficulties. She'll no longer be only a few blocks away. Maybe her youngest daughter will move her to Toronto to be nearer to her. I find myself hoping this will be the case.

I once heard Margaret Laurence say that when one reaches a certain age, there's no great tragedy in dying. But there can be great tragedy in the manner of the dying.

As I rise to take my cup and saucer to the sink, I keep seeing one of those dolls on her bed. The one wearing the Black Watch.

A Good Turn

Bonnie Thomas lay back in her moss-green bathtub and closed her eyes, not in relaxation, though that was her aim, but to try to rationalize her behaviour. The bathroom with its hanging pots of ivy was like an oasis in the new house that still seemed alien to her.

They'd moved in only last month, and already Brad was away on one of his far-too-many business trips. She'd jumped at the chance when the next door neighbours, the Hendersons, had invited her to their noisy big house-party. She shouldn't have gone. She knew that now, now that sobriety had returned. Her watch had said three-thirty when she'd taken it off. Probably almost four o'clock now.

Bonnie tensed at a sudden crackling sound. Must be one of those noises all new houses make, she thought. The girls wouldn't be up. She'd checked on them when she'd returned home a few minutes ago, and they'd been sleeping soundly. Twin, blonde, eleven-year-old angels. Somehow the sight of them had made her feel unclean.

Don't be silly, she told herself. After all, it was only a few kisses. It wasn't anything really serious. A bit of groping. She'd just been feeling a little too adventuresome. No, that wasn't it. Face it, she told herself, you had too much to drink — as usual. She shouldn't have had that fourth one. Or was it the fifth? Brad had warned her more than once her drinking was getting out of control. Bonnie rubbed her face with the green and white washcloth, but she couldn't rub away the guilt. Shameful embraces sneaked in the upstairs hall behind another woman's back, a woman who had befriended her. Steve Henderson probably thought her ready, willing, and waiting. The idea of his being right next door frightened her now. What an idiot she'd been! On top of everything else, she had no business leaving the girls alone. If Brad knew that, he'd …

Another creaking sound broke the stillness. It sounded like a footstep. Had she remembered to lock the front door? She'd been pretty tipsy. She could have forgotten. Bonnie stared at the pale green panels of the bathroom door. "Melanie!" she called. "Madeline!" Everything was deadly quiet. Bonnie sensed her body growing cold within the warmth of the water. She held the washcloth against her face, trying to control her terror. "Maddie!" she shouted again. Utter silence. Then another noise. " Mel!" she cried at the top of her lungs. How could her girls sleep so soundly! Slowly, she removed the wet washcloth from her face. Looking up, she saw the brass doorknob on the bathroom door turning. For a few moments, she remained frozen. Then it struck her. The girls were all alone with whoever was out there. She had to go to them.

When Bonnie climbed out of the tub and reached for her towel, she saw her heavy blue suede jacket lying atop the rest of her clothes on the floor — directly beneath the doorknob. Of course! That was it. She'd hung the heavy jacket over the knob in her hurry to get into the tub. She must have looked up just as it fell. Too soon to see the jacket, but just in time to see the knob turn. Well, it had certainly given her a turn — perhaps one in the right direction. From now on she'd change her ways. Turn for a change to reliable, refreshing, good old *aqua vita*.

Sam's Specialty

Sam Carleton fed another log into the hungry mouth of his pot-bellied stove before returning to his rocker — and his worries about his son. The rascal sure knew how to charm a wife. Trouble was, it was somebody else's wife he was charming.

His son Larry along with his daughter-in-law Bonnie had arrived early this morning. They'd brought another young couple with them — the Corbettes. Sam had sent the four of them to the grocery store with a lengthy list, but showing off his culinary skills was the last thing on his mind. Why couldn't Bonnie see what was going on right under her nose? Such a sweet girl, always thinking about others. Even trying to play Cupid to find him a mate. Not that he was totally opposed to her scheming. It would be good to have someone to share his life with again. Elva would have wanted that for him. Taking early retirement had helped. That and keeping busy managing this lodge in Muskoka. The tourist cabins kept him busy in the summer. Now the place was blanketed in snow and he whiled away the days painting and repairing them in preparation for next season. He was less lonely than he'd been in the city. The surrounding evergreens were a kind of company. They were also the reason for the presence of the four young people today. The were here on a Christmas tree hunting expedition.

Hearing a car outside, Sam hurried to the window and watched as the girls piled out of Dan Corbette's red station wagon. Rita began at once to play the coquette. Laughing, she lobbed a snowball at Larry and ran to duck behind the woodpile. As she peeked out, her black hair glistened in the morning sun, and her brown eyes flashed an invitation. Sam was forced to admit it wasn't difficult to see why his son found her attractive.

Bonnie wasn't helping matters. She seemed to be paying no attention whatsoever to their shenanigans. A person would think she'd been married a dozen years instead of just two. When she began lifting a big bag of groceries from the back of the wagon, Sam took his mackintosh from its hook by the door and went out to help.

"How come Larry's driving?" he asked her. "Where's Dan?"

"That camera nut," she replied, "made us drop him off back by the creek so he could do something he's going to call 'Study in Black and White'. Rita says he's been doing a lot of still-life lately."

Maybe he should catch his wife in action instead, Sam thought, but he made no comment. Rita and Larry were still chasing each other around the yard like two children just let out of school.

"Why don't you join those two," Sam suggested. "They seem to be having a lot of fun."

"I'd rather help you put this stuff away," Bonnie replied. "In fact, I'd like to make lunch for us, if that's okay with you."

"Fine," her father-in-law agreed. He was looking out the window again. Dan had returned, camera slung around his neck, but it was obvious the two hadn't noticed him. After a lucky shot that sent her yellow toque flying, Rita tackled Larry and was trying to wash his face with snow. Dan Corbette stood watching them, his expression stony. He was a good looking fellow, Sam thought, with his curly brown hair and bright blue eyes. Too bad he was so overweight.

Dan came in and placed his camera carefully on top of the maple bookshelf. "Fantastic scenery around here, Mr. Carleton. Absolutely fantastic."

"Please … call me Sam," the older man murmured, barely taking his eyes off the scenery outside — the scenery Dan should be studying.

The silence was broken only by the sound of Bonnie's luncheon preparations.

"Dan, call those two in to eat, will you?" she asked at last.

Sam was still standing by the window. He saw Larry bending towards Rita, assuming a kissing position. "Don't get up, Dan," he said in a rush. "I'll call them." He hurried out without his coat.

Rita seemed surprised at the brusqueness of his summons. She retrieved her yellow toque from a snow bank, pulled it over her wet black hair, and headed for the lodge. Sam held Larry's arm to keep him from following her.

"How long have you and Bonnie known the Corbettes?" he asked.

"A few months. The girls work in the same insurance office. Why?"

"Well … because …" Sam could feel his face flush.

"Because what?"

"Rita seems to be pretty flirtatious with you."

Larry chuckled. "Flirtatious. What a quaint word." He threw a comradely arm across his father's shoulders. "You know what they say, Dad. Passion is the fashion. Anyway, Bonnie doesn't seem to care, so why should you?"

"I'm serious, Larry. I'd hate to see anything go wrong …"

"Dad, there's nothing to worry about. Anyway, aren't you the man they used to call Casanova Sam? Maybe I'm just a chip off the old block."

Sam looked down at the snow-packed ground. The old nickname brought back memories. He'd remained a bachelor longer than most men. When he'd finally married at thirty-five, a few habits from his single days remained. One of them was occasionally treating women from his office to lunch. Elva had been unable to reach him the first time little Larry took sick. Turned out to be nothing but a stomach ache from eating whipped cream, but it taught Sam a lesson.

The enticing aroma of corn fritters and country-style sausages greeted them as they entered the lodge. "Smells good, Bonnie," Sam remarked.

"Hope it tastes good. I'm a little out of practice. Too many frozen dinners with both of us working."

"Rita's a good cook," said Dan. "Too good — as you can see by my waistline." He reached for a slice of bread but dropped his hand quickly as Sam bent his head to say grace.

Bonnie noticed his action. She should have warned him, she reflected. Perhaps he should be warned about something else as well. But jealousy was a new and entirely unwelcome emotion for her. She wasn't sure how to handle it. Maybe she was just imagining things. Larry liked people, liked having a good time. She had to trust him, had to make him know that she trusted him. He loved her as much as she loved him. She was certain of that.

Over coffee, they discussed plans for finding their Christmas trees. "Go up the north slope past the trail that leads to the old Ormsby house," said Sam. "Rick Ormsby owns all the land up that way, and he told me it would be okay for you to take a couple of trees. The north slope is covered thick with spruce."

"Let's get going," urged Larry. "Better wear an extra scarf, Bonnie. There's a wind coming up."

"You three go on ahead," she replied. "I'll help Dad with the dishes." She'd show Larry she trusted him. She wasn't going to spoil things between them by being overly possessive.

Sam pushed back his chair. "I can do these up in no time. You go along with them, Bonnie. I'll have dinner ready when you get back."

Larry, too, tried to get her to change her mind, but she refused. Sam felt like shaking her. Was she blind? Couldn't she see what was going on?

They donned their coats, Dan slung his camera over one shoulder, and the three of them set out.

"Don't forget the saw," Sam called after them. "I left it on top of the woodpile."

When she finished drying the dishes, Sam urged Bonnie to join the others. Instead, she picked up a book and curled up on the big green leather sofa. Sam studied her. Such a pretty girl, small boned and dainty. Naturally curly blond hair. Big blue eyes fringed with dark lashes. But those big eyes were missing a lot. Was there any way he could approach the subject? Best friends, he could say, are not always to be trusted. No, that wouldn't do at all. He picked up a magazine, sat down in his rocker, and idly leafed through it. Then he went out to chop some wood.

When he returned it was almost four o'clock and Bonnie was getting ready to leave. "Tell them I'm making my famous rice casserole for dinner," he said.

Just as Bonnie opened the door, Rita came hurtling in, face scratched, brown eyes brimming with tears. "Dan's lost!" she cried. "We've been searching and calling ever since we found the trees we wanted."

Sam helped her to a chair. "Take it easy. How did you get those scratches?"

"I don't know. Must have run into some brambles or something. Never mind me. We've got to find Dan. It'll soon be dark. He doesn't have a good sense of direction."

"Where's Larry?" demanded Bonnie.

"He's looking for Dan." Rita turned to Sam. "What are we going to do? This is all my fault. If I'd been paying attention …"

"I have an idea," Sam cut in. "You two stay here." He took his cap and mackintosh and headed for his workshop in the garage. He rummaged about until he found a small hatchet. Then he set off briskly towards the north slope. He recalled that the top of the hill afforded an excellent view of the Ormsby house. With its many gables and shingled turrets, the abandoned house made a picturesque sight — one a true camera bug would find irresistible. But the floors were so rotted out they wouldn't stand up to much weight.

The snow was just deep enough to make for hard going. Halfway up the slope he turned westward to follow the trail that led to the old house. He forged ahead as fast as he could, spurred on by the sting of snow against his face and the lengthening shadows.

As he drew near, Sam thought he heard a faint cry for help. He picked his way carefully up the sagging front steps and across the weather-beaten gray veranda. "Dan!" he called, peering into the gloomy interior.

"In here," came the reply. "By the window."

Sam made his way across the creaking floorboards of the living room.

"Am I glad to see you! I've been hollering myself blue in the face."

Sam couldn't hold back a grin. Dan was trapped in the window seat fronting the large bay window — both legs stuck up to his hips. Raising his hatchet, Sam began to chop away at the dusty boards. "Why did you climb up here in the first place?" he asked between blows.

"To get a good shot of that old fireplace."

"I figured you'd head here," Sam remarked as Dan rubbed his newly freed legs and made jokes about going on a diet. "This house is well over a hundred years old. Rick Ormsby's going to see to it that it's torn down, but he keeps putting it off. Guess he hates to see it go. It's been in the family so long."

"Tell him I'll send him some pictures to remember it by. I know I got some good ones."

They met Larry on the way back to the lodge. "Why did you take off like that?" he demanded.

A moment passed before Dan answered. "I didn't think you two were likely to miss me."

"Rita's been carrying on like a mad woman. We'd better hurry."

Dan and Rita were soon snuggling up together on the big green sofa, lost in a world of their own. Sam glanced at his son. Larry was wearing a peculiar expression as he watched them — one that gave Sam an idea.

"You can serve your casserole now, Dad," Bonnie called as she set the last plate on the table.

"First I have to prepare my *specialite de la maison*," Sam replied. "The dessert. Larry, come out to the kitchen and help me."

Looking puzzled, his son followed him. He watched while his father poured out a pitcher of thick cream and whipped it into stiff peaks. "Fetch me those chocolate puddings from the fridge," he said.

"Okay, Dad, but no whipped cream for me. You know what it does to me."

"Take a little of it and then pretend to be sick. See what Bonnie does."

"Sounds crazy."

"Humor me. Go along with it."

Half an hour later, Larry was holding his stomach and moaning while a frantic Bonnie raced back and forth with cold compresses for his forehead as he lay stretched out on the sofa. "Poor darling," she was murmuring. "Here. Rest your head in my lap. Dad, do you think we should call a doctor?"

"No. He used to get a stomach ache from whipped cream when he was a kid. Guess we both forgot. He'll be fine in a little while, you'll see."

Bonnie was still fussing over Larry like a new bride as they prepared for their return trip to the city. He was eating it up. They're going to be okay, Sam thought. More than okay.

"See you at Christmas, Dad. Guess we'll have to buy a tree from the corner lot. Think you could stay for a week this year? There's someone I'd like you to meet."

"Someone special?"

"Very special."

"You matchmaking again, Bonnie?"

"Well … you don't really mind, do you? She's a widow — and she's crazy about country living."

"What's her name?"

"Heather Martin. She's an attractive woman, nice personality too. Trust me, Dad."

"Oh, I do, Bonnie. Implicitly. I'll be there with bells on."

Sam chuckles as the four young people drive off. The snow has stopped falling. Everything looks white and peaceful. Funny, he muses, how things have a way of working out. But sometimes a little push in the right direction does no harm. Heather, hmm? Nice name, that.

Second Chance

I haven't seen her since my mother's funeral, so when my great-aunt phones Sunday morning to invite me for tea, I leave my husband Bob to his own devices and call on her.

She's frailer than I remember, and her sense of balance isn't good. As I feared, she gets out the shoebox full of old snapshots when we finish our tea and oatmeal cookies. Still, paper people can't run away, and neither can I — though I'd dearly love to.

The pictures are creased, dog-eared and yellowed with age.

"My cousin Min," she says, "just before she married that rich widower. Funny looking hat. The cloche was all the rage then."

The snapshots move from her trembling hand to mine. Three bearded men standing self-consciously beside a steam engine, dressed in their Sunday best, fedoras at rakish angles. A group of children at the beach, sand castles still defying both the waves and the years. Two young bloods leaning on shovels, polka-dotted hankies knotted at their necks. A pretty flapper shielding her eyes from the sun. Some pictures have fancy black borders. These distant relatives have old-fashioned names: Myrtle, Noble, Effie, Roy, Loyal ... how my great-aunt remembers them all is quite beyond me. Finally, inevitably, we come to the one I've been both dreading and looking forward to. My father, the Libyan oil fields man, the man I've tried so hard to hate, the man my mother refused to talk about. I've thought about him a lot, but I've seen him only once. At least I think I saw him. I can't be certain.

I hold the faded snapshot, searching as I've searched before for some clue, some answer to the puzzle of paternity. Do men feel no ties to the children they produce? He walked out on my mother when I was a baby.

"Maybe he wanted a son," I joked bitterly as soon as I was old enough to be told.

I move the picture even closer and study it intensely. The face is handsome in an early matinee idol sort of way. Black hair, thick and wavy, bee-stung lips, something haunted looking about the dark eyes. All in all, the male equivalent of my own face.

My great-aunt is staring at me in a most peculiar way. I put my father's picture back into the box. Face down.

"I think I should tell you," she says suddenly.

"Tell me what?"

"About your father ... why he left. I promised your mother I'd be quiet, but now that she's gone ..." She stops, removes her eyeglasses, and dabs at her eyes with a lace-edged hankie.

I wish I could feel more sorrow about my mother's passing, but we were never really close. There always seemed to be a sort of invisible wall between us. Tell me what? I'm wondering, consumed with curiosity. But I control myself until my great-aunt speaks again. Eighty-seven year old ladies have earned the right to take their time. Finally, she begins.

"In those days they didn't talk about it openly, you see. Not the way they do now, on all the talk shows and everything. Your mother and Ellen preferred to keep it a deep dark secret. Even from you. Especially from you. But Lisa, you must have suspected. I did. Even before I surprised them that time."

"Suspected?"

"That they were ... you know ... what's the word? Lesbians."

I'm stunned into silence. The woman I called Aunt Ellen when I was little and my mother? Impossible. Ellen died from a ruptured appendix a few months after I was married. I never got to know her very well. She was a real estate agent and out most evenings. I thought it was a simple matter of economics that she and my mother shared the house.

My great-aunt's hand rests lightly on my shoulders.

"This must be a shock for you, Lisa. Maybe I shouldn't have said anything. But I can't believe you didn't have any idea ..."

"I didn't. But I'm glad you told me. It explains a lot. I always felt like a stranger at home. Almost like an intruder ..."

"Your father was generous in his support payments, that I know. I never understood for the life of me why your mother felt so vindictive. To my way of thinking, it should have been the other way around. Well, sometimes we can't even begin to understand the actions of others — even those dearest to us."

Impulsively, I hug her, surprising both of us.

"I'm so glad you told me, Auntie. You know, I thought I saw my father eight years ago — on my wedding day. A man was lingering outside the Registry Office who looked ... I don't know ... like me somehow. But my mother hustled Bob and me into the car so fast ..."

"It *was* your father. Do you want to get in touch with him?"

"Yes. Yes, I do."

"He wrote me just after your mother's funeral. He enclosed his current address just in case you were interested. He wanted to see you, but he never would have felt comfortable when Ellen was around. Then, too, he was out of the country a lot of the time. Later, he said he felt it was too late, that you wouldn't want to see him. I thought the world of your mother, Lisa, but I think she was misguided. She should have told you the truth."

I look down at the envelope she hands me. The address is on the upper left hand corner. He lives in a city only a few hours' drive away. Inside, there's a telephone number. I can't wait to get home and call it. Can't wait to tell him he's going to have a grandchild in six weeks. Maybe it'll be a little girl. I wouldn't let them tell me. Nevertheless, boy or girl, it'll be sort of like having a second chance — for both of us.

Sweet Comic Valentine

Helen was dusting her ten-year-old son's room when she found it. An expensive valentine with real red satin covering a huge heart surrounded by pink cherubs and white lace. *I Love You* proclaimed the otherwise spotless interior of the card.

Oh, Kevin, I love you too, she thought, her previous anger rapidly dissipating in the heat of the red satin heart. So what if he never cleaned his room. She wasn't the only mother who had to cope with that problem. It was one of the most common complaints she heard when she got together with other members of her Parents Without Partners group.

She finished tidying the maple desk, ran a dust mop over the varnished floor until it grew a beard and closed the door to her son's room, hoping she hadn't spoiled his surprise for her. With Kevin, all show of affection had to come from cards and presents. He had never been a demonstrative child, and her attempts at physical contact with him were invariably rebuffed. But he was good at remembering special days; Helen still had every card he had ever given her. All the others, however, had been homemade. This one must have cost him more than a week's allowance.

At noon, Kevin returned from the park, his face glowing from the cold, his brown eyes gleaming with anticipation.

"It sure seems funny having Valentine's Day on a Saturday, doesn't it?" he commented over a bowl of tomato soup.

Helen reached out to push a cluster of damp black curls away from his eyes, and he promptly pulled away from her.

"Who won the big snowball fight?" she asked.

"Tracy said the girls did, but we did really. It's just there are more of them than us."

She sat down across from him. "When I was young," she said, "boys weren't allowed to hit girls. It was absolutely against all the rules."

Kevin reached for a second handful of soda biscuits to crumble over his soup. "No kidding! Things have sure changed, haven't they, Mom."

"They certainly have. No more biscuits, Kevin. You've got more soda crackers than soup now."

As soon as they finished lunch, Kevin made a strange request. "Can I put on my Sunday clothes?" he asked.

"May I. And whatever for?"

The rest of the boy's face turned as red as his cheeks. "I want to go over to Tracy's house."

"Why?"

"I … I've got something for her." Taking a deep breath, he added. "It's a valentine. I bought one for her."

For a moment, Helen was speechless. Wordlessly, she regarded her son across the crumb-littered tablecloth.

"But didn't you just see her this morning?" she asked at last.

"Sure. But that's different. I've never seen her alone. That's how I want to give her the card. When we're alone."

Helen smiled. Her son looked so very young — and so completely under the spell of the blonde and dainty Tracy she couldn't refuse him. He had never before shown any interest in any girl. "No playing on the way home in your good clothes," she admonished.

"Nope."

In a flash, he was off. She heard him bustling about, getting ready, brushing his teeth without being told. She stared after him as he left, handsome in his beige corduroy jeans and blue cotton shirt, brown eyes shining and eager as he waved good-bye. In his right hand he carried the card, safely hidden in one of his Superman comic books.

Helen turned her attention to the pile of their combined breakfast and lunch dishes.

She heard him return when she was putting the last glass into the cupboard above the sink. "Back so soon?" she called out. There was no reply.

Puzzled, she hung up the tea towel and went into the front hall of their apartment.

Kevin rushed past her, but she caught up with him just as he reached his room. "What happened?" she asked.

He looked at her, eyes no longer eager.

"What happened, Kevin? Didn't Tracy like the card?"

"She tore it up, Mom. She tore it all to pieces." The words came out all in a rush before he took refuge in his room, shutting the door firmly behind him.

Helen stood very still outside the closed door. Should she give him that chocolate bar she'd been saving as a special treat? No. She'd read somewhere that food offered as a panacea led to obesity in later life. Maybe she should just leave him to sort it out for himself. Life was full of hurdles … of pain. She of all people knew that. It was Kevin's father who'd wanted out — not her. The boy might as well get used to the ways of the world.

But finally the heavy silence beyond the door was more than she could bear. Impetuously, she flung it open and rushed headlong into the room.

Kevin was standing by the window, looking oddly formal. She surprised him with a full-length bear hug, a hug so tight he had no chance whatever of escaping it.

But the funny thing was, he didn't even try.

Boxes

He was thirty-six, but his daily confrontations with mirrors told him he looked fifty-six. The old couple looked about eighty. Just the right age to be his grandparents.

He'd first discovered them in their ground floor apartment when his car had broken down and he'd had to walk the six blocks to work. They always sat side by side in ancient armchairs, staring out with fading eyes at the passing scene.

Now he walked whenever weather permitted — just to get a glimpse of them before settling down in his tiny bookkeeper's box of an office, and before returning to his square and dingy furnished room each night.

Even though they had never so much as exchanged eye contact, they had become his grandparents. He'd invented their histories, where they'd met, how they'd courted, when they'd wed. Each morning he added more embroidery work until the tapestries of their histories were rich with details. After a few weeks, the background of their lives was more familiar to him than his own.

His own. That was a laugh. His background was a mystery, a cipher. Abandoned in a railway station. In a shoe box. Sounded like something out of a Victorian melodrama. As a child, he had tried to think of the last foster home as a real home, but it hadn't worked. He'd been a complete disappointment to them — like all the others. Neither strong nor even passably good-looking; and always too anxious to please. So anxious he seemed to appear unnatural — even in his own eyes. He wasn't even clever with figures. He'd become a bookkeeper only because there was nothing else he could do. He had to work extra hard at it — the way he had to work extra hard at everything he tried.

His willingness to put every effort into finding companionship met with no success. When he wanted a woman, he had to pay for one. Male companionship was out of the question. He kept up with the sports scene, but nobody ever listened when he commented on it. He frequently felt he was locked into some sort of invisible box. Even in the restaurant where he habitually took his meals the waitresses looked straight through him, indifferent as the tasteless food.

It wasn't only their eyes that were beginning to fade, he thought, one morning when he passed his "grandparents'" apartment. They both wore the same sort of rimless spectacles, but their bodies seemed a little more frail, a little less distinct each day. The old lady invariably wore a grey dress, the old man a suit of the same shade. Both had silver hair, cut short. Though his gesture was never returned, he nodded to them each morning on his way to work and every afternoon on his return. It became the most important part of his daily routine.

He recoiled as though from a body blow the afternoon his grandparents disappeared. He came to a full stop in front of their apartment, overcome by a sense of loss, uncertainty furrowing his brow.

When a flamboyantly dressed middle-aged man and woman emerged from the front door, loaded with cardboard cartons, he screwed up his courage and took a tentative step towards them. "The old couple," he began apologetically, "… the old couple who lived here … is one of them ill or something?"

The middle-aged pair exchanged a should-we-tell-him look. He knew the look. People used it often in his presence. They invariably ended up not telling him. He waited, eyes beseeching. The woman was the first to speak. She appeared to be having trouble keeping a straight face. "They were dummies," she said. "When we moved out of here we had to leave several valuable antiques behind, including our furniture. We thought our belongings would be safer if the place looked inhabited. We had the lights timed to go off and on."

The man chuckled. "We're artists," he added. "We made them ourselves. They were really life-like, weren't they!"

For what seemed a very long time, Harold was too stunned to answer. "They looked so *real*," he managed at length. Then he noticed that the stranger seemed to be studying him intently. "I'm a photographer," said the man, "and you have a most interesting face. May I ask you your name?"

"It's Harold — Harold Westover."

"Well, Harold, would you consider sitting for me? I'm currently engaged in a special project, and your face would be perfect for it."

Harold could scarcely believe his ears. "I'd be happy to oblige," he stammered.

"Good. I'm Sanford Wells, and this is my wife, Bettina. She'll give you all the details. We're going to be seeing a lot of each other."

As Bettina smiled and shook his hand the world seemed to Harold Westover a much friendlier place.

A Book By Its Cover

The last time I called I had a tough time convincing her everything was fine. My mother always could read me like a book. When I was a kid, she swore my nose turned red whenever I lied to her. I'm seventeen now, but she can still tell. Even on the phone. Even long distance.

Right now I'm on my way to see my tough old landlady, and I'm not looking forward to it. She's at least forty, and she dyes her hair bright red. She puts green crap all over her eyelids, and she wears the most godawful orange lipstick. Her eyebrows are orange too. They look like fuzzy caterpillars crawling across her forehead. She has a deep voice, a voice my dad always calls a whiskey voice. Her name is Mrs. Harvey. I don't know what her first name is. She should be called Mrs. Leopard because that's what she looks like in those spotted pants and tops she's always wearing. She's tall and skinny and has a feral look.

Feral is the perfect word for her. I read a lot, and I've always been good at English composition. I'm not good with people though. I'm really afraid of approaching Mrs. Harvey. But the alternative of giving up and going home is even more unattractive. I can just hear my mother saying, "Well, you can't say we didn't warn you. We'll wire you the money to come home. We know what's best for you, Barbie."

* * *

I hate it when they call me Barbie. Makes me feel like that stupid doll I used to spend hours dressing and undressing. My names's Barbra — with only two "a"s. Like the famous singer. I changed it to that spelling myself. Only I'm going to be a famous writer, not a singer.

I'm the youngest in the family, so maybe that's why they've always treated me like a baby, always acted like they know me better than I know myself. "There's no future in writing," my mom argues. Just because she has a friend who's forever scribbling poems and short stories and never selling any of them. But it won't be like that with me. Not if I can go to that university out west that has the good creative writing course. And just because my mom wanted to be a nurse, that doesn't mean it's the right path for me to follow. I can't give up now. I just can't.

My knees are trembling as I descend the staircase from my third-floor furnished room. But I have to face my landlady sooner or later. I just wish she was a nicer person.

We had a terrible fight the day I told my parents what I wanted to do. They own a chip wagon back in my hometown and every summer I had to serve customers from it while my friends basked in the sun or played volleyball on the beach. At school they always teased me about smelling like salt and vinegar. I was in an unbearable situation. They say it's good for writers to suffer, but there has to be a limit.

"You'll work here till you finish high school," insisted my dad. "Just like your brothers before you. This is a family business."

"I've only got a year to go to finish high," I retorted. "I can go to Toronto and make it on my own. I'll support myself."

"You'll never be able to do it, Barbie," cautioned my mother. "It's a tough world out there. You have no idea how tough."

"I don't care," I yelled. "I'll get my diploma without selling one more damned old greasy chip!"

My mom raised her hand and I thought she was going to smack me. "Our chips are not greasy!" she shouted. "And you watch your mouth, my girl."

I can't help smiling now, thinking of the way my parents defended their chips. My dad still has the clipping from a weekend paper saying theirs were voted the best chips in Southern Ontario. It's framed and hanging in their wagon. That day ended happily — for me, anyway. My parents ended up promising me I could follow my dreams to become a writer if I could finish my last year of high school on my own.

Tonight the landlady looks like a polyester orange and white leopard. As I stand in her kitchen doorway, she takes a swig from her bottle of beer and eyes me up and down. The spiral of blue smoke from her cigarette drifts up towards the tobacco-stained ceiling.

"Rent was due yesterday," she says.

"I know, Mrs. Harvey, but if you could just let me have a few days …"

"No extensions. Tole ya that when ya moved in." Her green eyes below the drawn on orange eyebrows are fixed on me, unblinking. A wildcat.

I swallow hard. "I'm expecting a cheque in tomorrow's mail," I lie.

"Yeah, yeah. I heard that one a hunnert times."

I pull at the band of my gold-plated watch. It'll be hell getting to classes on time, but it's all I have left. I've pawned everything of any value since I lost my waitressing job. Lost it for serving cherry cheesecake up a customer's nose. I wasn't sorry either. The big slob asked for it, every day for a week. So finally, I lost it. The owner of the restaurant wouldn't listen when I told him the customer is not always right. I have my rights, too.

"I didn't hear him insult you," the owner protested.

"That's because he was smart enough to whisper. Nobody else heard him either."

But my explanation had been in vain. Losing that job was tough. The tips were good, and I could easily have made it through to graduation.

My landlady is examining the watch. "This aint worth shit," she says.

I'm tempted to fib, to try to convince her it's valuable. I have nothing else to bargain with. From stories I've heard, if I were a good looking jock … well, let's just say I'd be in a better position for bargaining. A couple of winks, a few promises and I'd be able to talk her into all the extensions I needed. I've heard some of the guys joking about her in the hallways.

Mrs. Harvey is staring at me. "Why doncha go on back home, Barbra. You tole me your folks wanted you to keep on working for them. Why doncha do it till you finish school? A job's a job." She stubs out her cigarette in an overflowing ashtray. She sure doesn't pay any attention to what the surgeon general has to say.

"Mrs. Harvey, you don't understand. I totally hate working in the chip wagon. All that hot, smelly grease. It's the worst job in the world. The absolute pits."

"Yer lucky ya have parents willin' to send ya to school. You young people today don't know how lucky you are, and that's a fact."

I'm sorry now that I ever confided in her. She starting to sound like my parents. But she's examining the wristwatch again, and my hopes rise.

"I guess fryin' potatoes aint much of a job at that," she says. "Must be a lousy way of makin' a living."

I don't contradict her, but my parents have made tons of money out of their chip wagon business by the river. Enough to buy a big red brick house and send all three of my brothers to university.

"Ya look about ready to cry, Barbra," she goes on. "Sit down and take a load off. Mebbe we can figure something out. I know how tough it is to get through the teens at home. My ole man threw me outta the house for wearing lipstick. You only got a couple of months to go to finish school, right?"

"Yeah, but I lost my job, and you're right about that watch. It's not worth much."

"How'd ya lose yer job?"

When I tell her, she surprises me by breaking up, laughing and coughing at the same time. "Good on ya, girl! You got spunk. I oughta try that method when them young guys try to talk me into waiting fer the rent."

"Then those stories aren't true," I blurt out, unthinking.

"What stories? No, don't bother. I can guess. Just because I felt sorry for them once or twice. But no matter."

"But they shouldn't talk about you like that. Next time I hear them, I'm telling them so."

She grins. "Are you tryin' ta change the subject, Barbra?"

I decide to be totally honest, to throw myself on her mercy. "If you could just give me a week …"

She leans toward me over the kitchen table, face cupped in her hands, deep in thought. "I have it!" she cries. "We'll go to the restaurant and get your job back. We'll threaten to charge them with — what's that word? Yeah, sexual harassment."

"No, that won't work. Thanks, but no. The other waitresses wouldn't testify for me. They didn't like me all that much. Anyway, it would be too hard to prove."

Mrs. Harvey goes into her thinking mode again. "How about if I give you a job?" she wonders out loud. "Work for me and live rent free. Hey! I'm a poet and didn't know it."

I laugh politely, but I'm all ears — especially about the rent free part. "What do I have to do?"

"Don't worry, I'll keep you busy. It's getting too much for me here. My husband used to help, but he took off for parts unknown a year ago. You can help with the laundry, change the beds. I'll even feed you. Mebbe we can put a little meat on them bones."

"Look who's talking!" I tease. "Mrs. Harvey, I don't know how to thank you. Is there anything you want me to do tonight?"

"Yeah, you can start calling me Dorothy. Now get up them stairs and hit the books. I expect you to get straight A's."

I'm starting up the stairs when she catches up with me. "You forgot your watch, Barbra," she says, handing it to me.

"Mrs. Harvey … Dorothy, you are not a leopard. You are a pussycat."

Leaving her looking pleased but puzzled, I race up the stairs to my room, to my books, to my independence, to my future.

The Patchwork Comforter

The gulls are wheeling in perilously close, high-pitched cries increasing, sharp beaks threatening. Elaine wants to cry with them. Still, the healing tears refuse to come.

"Mom, turn more this way," urges her daughter Debra. "That's it. Now hang on till I focus."

Hang on, Elaine tells herself, gripping the cold wet railing of the ferry. She recalls a toy camera someone gave Debra on a long-ago birthday. One click of the shutter and a gray felt mouse was hurled at the unwitting subject. Elaine had confiscated it, fearing it could precipitate a heart attack. But heart attacks are not like that, she thinks now. They come when least expected … strike without warning on a sunny June morning.

This trip to Manitoulin Island is her mother's idea. " Debra can drive us," she'd insisted. "Be good for you to get away."

But Elaine feels confused, disoriented. Her life has blown up in her face, and she doesn't know where any of the pieces are. She can't even begin to imagine a life without Bill.

Debra has taken the picture and is heading for the stern of the ferry, long blonde hair flying in the wind. Watching her, Elaine thinks she looks more like nineteen than twenty-nine. Elaine starts to follow her, but her daughter turns to tell her to stay where she is. "I want one of you and Grandma together," she explains.

Elaine returns to the railing and stares down at the crisscrossing blue and white lines of the receding wake. The deep water is magnetic, inviting. She finds herself recalling the trip she and Bill took to the Island when Debra was nine — the same age as Elaine had been when her family left Manitoulin for good. Bill had spent most of his time in the bar on that trip, while she tried vainly to amuse their child, her irritation growing. When finally he'd left his new-found cronies to join them, mother and daughter presented a united front of silence. But Bill had always been able to make her laugh. All it had taken that time was his special rendition of *I Love You Truly*. She'd given in somewhere around the words, *"fades into dreams when I feel you are near."*

Her mother is tugging at her arm. "Debra wants us to look towards that white ladder," she says. "Try to smile. We haven't got one good picture of the two of us."

Elaine moves her head in the required direction. Debra is so like her father — even when it comes to taking pictures. Nobody can rush her. Each shot has to be just so. But right now, Elaine know her daughter is only going through the motions to try to keep her occupied, keep her from thinking of the empty years ahead.

Debra lowers her camera. Mona, who never poses with her cane, picks it up from the deck and they make their way into the nearest lounge.

"Grandma, how long is it since you've been back to the Island?" asks her granddaughter.

The old lady draws her sparse white eyebrows together. "Must be going on twelve years now. Your grandpa and I went for a week, but we didn't see any of our old friends. Not even the McDermotts. Spent all our time fishing. After he passed on I didn't feel like making the trip anymore."

At least you were able to celebrate your golden anniversary, Elaine thinks. That's more than Bill and I got. A lot more.

Debra goes on asking questions, urging responses, doing her best to keep the conversation from flagging. Her words circle Elaine's head like the gulls, only now they are soft gray birds, brushing dark wings against her ears. Nothing seems to make any sense. Nothing has made any sense since the Sunday Bill died behind the locked door of their bathroom. June the thirteenth. A little over two months ago. Ironic. She'd never been superstitious about the number thirteen. They'd been getting ready to go out that morning, she with her sketch pad, he with his camera.

For weeks afterwards, she'd roamed about their empty house, wondering when she'd wake up, wondering when Bill would come and tell her it was all a joke.

"Mom, isn't there anything you'd like? How about a coffee?"

"Yes … coffee. Fine." She stares at the porthole's round green eye, remembering Bill's face, his laugh, the special way he tousled her hair whenever she was worried or upset.

It seems a long time later when her mother's voice cuts into her thoughts. "Your coffee's getting cold."

Like an obedient child she lifts the tepid liquid to her lips and takes a few sips. For every cup of happiness, she thinks, you drink a cup of sorrow.

"This cousin Lottie we're going to visit," says Debra, "where does she live again? I like driving when I know where I'm going, but it's hard when …"

"Your grandma knows the way," Elaine interrupts. "We used to go there when I was a kid."

"She's on a farm just outside of Kilorough," Mona says. "Lives there all alone. Said in her letter she'd be glad to put us up. Said if I've forgotten the way we could ask anybody in Kilorough how to get to her place. Last time your grandpa and I were there, she used us real good. Her husband was there then, and two of her sons were still at home.

Used us real good. Pure Island talk. It used to irritate Elaine. "I wouldn't know Lottie if I passed her on the street," she confesses.

"Lottie was a good-looking woman. Black hair. Big brown eyes. Nice dresser, too. And always cheerful. I expect she's changed some."

Elaine stares at her mother's profile. One china blue eye is directed unseeingly past her. Like a blue marble. The result of a long-ago accident. But Elaine has more than once seen tears fall from that eye. She wonders now why she herself can't cry.

They return to the deck and at length they are able to discern the misty outline of Manitoulin Island looming ahead. Mona refuses to take the ferry's elevator, so Debra helps her down the metal steps. Elaine follows them into the dank bowels of the ferry. When they are seated in the car, she glances across at her daughter's rigid profile. Debra has never liked driving over water. But Elaine is in no condition to take over the wheel.

Twilight is falling when they finally turn into the long dirt lane that leads to Lottie's farmhouse. They've asked directions three times and gotten lost twice. Near the sagging gray barn a large tractor stands silhouetted against the sky. Debra parks their Buick beside another piece of farm machinery that looks like some sort of medieval torture rack.

"This place gives me the creeps," she says, taking the key from the ignition. "It's probably okay in the house, but it sure looks deserted out here."

"I hope Lotties's home." Mona sounds worried. "There doesn't seem to be much light coming from the house. My eyes aren't too good anymore, but … Good Lord! What was that?"

Debra puts an arm around her grandmother's shoulders. "It's nothing. Just a dog howling somewhere. Or maybe the wind."

They climb the rickety wooden steps of the side porch. Debra opens the screen door and pounds on the wooden one behind it. A bolt of sudden lightning splits the horizon to their left.

"Not an electric storm!" protests Mona. "Island storms are terrible. So much rock …"

Her voice is lost in the ensuing clap of thunder.

"Why doesn't she answer!" Debra wails. She pounds again on the door. "I don't like this. Maybe we'd better go back to the car before it starts to rain."

Elaine remains motionless. This trip wasn't my idea, she tells herself. Let them make all the decisions.

Abruptly, the door swings open. The person facing them looks as much male as female — gray hair cropped short, weathered brown skin, faded plaid shirt and blue jeans.

"Lottie?" Mona's voice trembles with something more than age.

"Mona." Lottie's voice is flat, expressionless. "You must be Elaine," she goes on.

"And my granddaughter Debra," Mona offers. After another great clap of thunder, she adds, "Shall we bring in our bags, Lottie?"

With a monochromatic "yes" Lottie stands aside to let her enter. Elaine and Debra fetch the suitcases, making it back inside just as the rain begins.

The four women sit down in the large kitchen and regard one another across the worn oilcloth covering the square table. It's patterned with faded yellow roses. The only illumination comes from a dim, centrally suspended light bulb.

Mona clears her throat and rubs the handle of her wooden cane. "So you're living here all alone now, Lottie."

"I get by. Get the pension. I do just fine."

"But don't you get nervous out here by yourself? You seem to be miles from any neighbors. Do you have a cat? Or a dog?"

"Nope. Don't much like animals."

An uncomfortable silence descends. Debra breaks it by asking, "Aren't you afraid of intruders? I mean away out here … all alone."

Wordlessly, Lottie points to the shotgun leaning against the wall in a shadowed corner by the living room door.

I should be trying to help, Elaine thinks, should be trying to change the direction of this conversation. But her throat is tight and dry. Her gaze rests for a time on the shotgun. Then she looks toward the dark, rain-slashed windows. And there is nothing she wants to say except let's go home. Only home isn't home anymore.

"I expect you'll be wanting a cup of tea before we go up," Lottie remarks. She rises to put the kettle on.

After they've eaten soggy, beige-colored cookies held together by sickly sweet pink icing, Lottie leads them upstairs to their assigned rooms. Elaine's is papered in faded stripes of brown broken by patterns of blue irises. She's read somewhere that the iris is a symbol for everlasting life. So much for symbols. The room has an odor of dust — as though no one has slept in it for years. She pulls off her white pants and gets under the musty-smelling covers wearing the rest of her clothes. She has no hope of sleep, but it will be a relief to no longer have to even try to function.

When the rain stops towards morning, a wind begins to howl around the corners of the old farmhouse. Like hordes of widows, Elaine thinks, howling for comfort. She prays for the release of tears. But her eyes remain open — and dry. Finally, she drifts into a troubled sleep.

When she wakes up, she wonders momentarily where she is. Then she remembers everything. She climbs stiffly out of the brown metal bed as the teakettle begins to whistle on the woodstove downstairs. Making her way along the cold linoleum floor of the hallway, she goes into the bathroom and splashes cold water over her face. She glances up at the mirror. Her blonde hair is a mess, but she doesn't bother to comb it.

Her mother's voice comes to her clearly when she's halfway down the stairs. "At least Bill went fast. You and I should be so lucky when our time comes, eh, Lottie?"

Elaine rushes forward and runs out of the house, slamming the screen door behind her. Just walk, she tells herself. Just walk and keep on walking.

Debra comes across the fields to get her. "Grandma doesn't mean any harm, Mom. That's just the way she talks. You know how she is. Come back to the house. Have a cup of Lottie's terrible instant coffee."

Lottie is talking to Mona in her strange monotone when they join them in the kitchen. "It's today we're having it. We have one every third Saturday of the month. At the community hall — seven miles away. I play piano, the others drums 'n violins. And one guitar. We all sing. Sell crafts too, things we make ourselves. People come from all over these parts. The three of you can come with me. Hanna McDermott's always there. She's an old friend of yours, isn't she, Mona?"

It's Lottie's longest speech since their arrival. Elaine looks at her mother whose cheeks are flushed with excitement. "Hanna McDermott! The McDermotts used to come to visit us practically every Sunday when we lived in Sandfield. You were just a baby, Elaine, you wouldn't remember. I must start getting ready. I'm glad I packed my new blue dress. Lottie, do you think there's enough hot water for me to have a bath? Fancy that! Hanna McDermott! I can't wait to see her after all these years. I'll wear my pearls. And my good earrings."

Elaine turns to her mother. Despite her seventy-five years, she looks oddly child-like in her anticipation. "Why don't you three go and I'll just stay here," she says.

"We can't leave you here alone," protests Debra. "Come on. Get ready. A musical afternoon. It might be fun."

"Don't expect too much," warns Lottie. "We don't play the kind of music you young folks go for."

When they leave the house, Lottie's wearing a navy-blue dress spotted with polka dots and sporting a large white bow at the neckline. She insists she'll drive them in her old Ford. Mona is resplendent in her blue silk, and Debra has switched from shorts to a red tube top with khaki jeans that flatter her trim figure.

"You look like Sheena, Queena the jungle," jokes Mona.

"You look like a real queen, Grandma. That's a beautiful shade of blue."

Elaine hasn't bothered to change. Yesterday's white pants and black tee shirt are good enough. She doesn't want to go. But staying here alone would be worse.

Lottie places a pork and bean casserole in the trunk of her car. "Pot luck dinner," she explains. "I'll stop by the general store in Kilorough so's you can pick up some cookies and a cake to bring. Maybe some pickles too. Hardly anybody brings good pickles."

The wooden structure of the community hall rises like an angular beehive of activity from a flat and treeless terrain. Men and women are carting covered dishes and artwork up the steep front steps, calling out greetings to newcomers as they arrive.

Lottie sets her casserole on the trestle table and goes immediately to the piano which sits grandly upon a raised platform at the far end of the hall. Other oldsters are already attacking bass, violin, guitar, and drums. The general cacophony as they tune up is drowned out only now and then by the high pitch of the talk going on around them. It reminds Elaine of the screaming gulls on the ferry.

The three visitors set down their purchased food and go to look over the crafts displayed on the narrow tables that line the walls of the large room. Sequined designs on squares of black velvet vie for attention with oil paintings of lopsided lighthouses and solid-looking waterfalls. There are miniature buildings made of matchsticks, toilet roll covers made in every possible design from clowns to princesses, and empty Javex bottles cut in half and filled with arrangements of dried weeds. There are homemade doll clothes and wooden carvings of animals of questionable identification. The jars of homemade preserves are also of questionable identification — except for the peaches.

"Wanna buy a ticket on a patchwork comforter?" asks a stout woman with a cigar box half full of change and bills on her lap. "A dollar each, or three for five dollars." She gestures towards the blanket tacked up on the wall above her table. "We're drawin' fer it right after we eat."

The visitors stare up at the conglomeration of quilted cotton scraps hanging above their heads. A riot of red and purple predominates, but there are rags of every color worked into the comforter in no discernible pattern. The whole thing is edged in a bilious green material.

"I don't think so," replies Elaine.

"No, thank you," murmurs Mona.

Debra shakes her head, claps one hand over her mouth, and moves rapidly ahead. Several hostile looks are directed their way.

"I'm sorry," Debra says as they move towards the stage. "I shouldn't have laughed. But I've never seen anything quite like that comforter."

"Do you recognize that tune?" asks Mona. "It sounds a little like *Swanee River*, but I don't know …"

"I think it's *Smoke Gets in Your Eyes*," Elaine replies.

Debra sits down beside them. "I think they're still warming up. Something tells me this is going to be a long day."

"Why don't we join the group over there for a few hands of euchre," Mona suggests. "You still remember how to play, Debra?"

"I think so. Anyway, I'll give it my best shot. How about you, Mom?"

"I couldn't concentrate on cards."

"We might as well try," Mona insists. "Might make the time go faster. I wish Hanna McDermott would get here. That's really why I came — to see her again."

They wander over to the card tables and after a time one of the women sets up an extra table to accommodate them. Debra's partner is an elderly man whose wife stands behind him fingering her white beads and watching with disapproval every move Debra makes.

"Would you like to take my place?" Debra finally offers.

"No, I'm fine right here. You two go ahead. I'll just watch — if you don't mind."

After she and her partner have lost two games running, Debra makes the foolish mistake of trumping her partner's ace.

"You two aren't likely to win a game in a month of Sundays," the wife crows, her satisfaction evident.

Promptly at five o'clock the food is put out and there is a great rush towards the tables. Instruments are abandoned and card games deserted. Paper plates are piled high with beans, salads, sandwiches, cold meats and cookies.

"Why do you suppose Hanna didn't show up?" Mona asks Lottie.

"She's often late. She has to drive in all the way from Millers Acres. But she usually gets here in time to eat and join us for the last concert of the day."

"You're going to play again?" asks Debra.

"Sure. We don't break up till ten-thirty or eleven. Sometimes it's twelve."

Trying to balance her paper plate and cane in one hand while she reaches for a piece of celery Mona spills potato salad over the front of her dress. Debra rushes to help her. "Come to the washroom with me, Grandma. I'll sponge it off."

Elaine sits stiffly on a chair apart from everyone. She looks down at the untouched food on the plate Debra has handed her. With a fork, she moves the beans around. Being at home in an empty house was bad, but this is infinitely worse. Lottie comes over demanding her attention. "Where's your mother? That's Hanna McDermott coming in right now."

A wiry little woman with steel-gray hair enters the room. She goes directly to the stout woman who was selling tickets on the patchwork comforter. "How'd we make out?" she enquires in a voice oddly loud for her size.

"Pretty good, Hanna. Thirteen bucks." The ticket vendor raises one chubby hand to her mouth to add words meant for Hanna's ears only.

Moments later, Mona and Debra return. Lottie leads the newcomer across to them. "I guess you remember this here lady, don't you, Hanna?"

The short woman lifts her chin and looks Mona up and down. "Only just vaguely," she replies and walks away.

Mona picks her way carefully across the room to a vacant chair where she sits with her cane across her knees, staring into space.

"God, did you see that!" cries Debra. "She snubbed Grandma."

"Go sit with her," says Elaine. "You're the only one who can help. We seem to rub each other the wrong way these days."

The music starts up again, and a few couples begin self-consciously to dance to it. Elaine feels suspended in another era. She doesn't know how long she's been sitting with her eyes closed when she becomes aware of a familiar melody. People are singing along in trembling sopranos and uncertain vibratos. Her throat constricts as she hears the age-old words. *I love you truly, truly dear. Life with its sorrows, life with its tears.*

Bill's smile materializes before her, then his teasing eyes, the way he'd hold one hand over his heart as he hammed up the words …

His heart.

She rises and pushes her way through a blurred ocean of tears to the outside of the community hall. Closing the heavy wooden door behind her, she sinks down on the steep steps and gives herself up to grief. But she isn't crying for herself alone. She's crying for the whole damn world … for all the random islands of human misery, scraping against each other, moving always towards the mirage of comfort.

The night is dark and starless. A scrap of black cloud hides the face of the moon. It's growing late. Time, Elaine decides, to go back inside. Time to face the music, however discordant.

Ice Cold Kindness

"**Good evening, ladies and gentlemen.** I want to thank you for inviting me to be your keynote speaker tonight. The Neighbours and Newcomers Club has always been important to me — especially since I was one of its founding members.

The minute I tasted our dessert, strawberry ice-cream, I put my prepared speech back into my bag. Because the dessert brought back memories — memories I would like to share with you.

Seventy years ago I first came to Canada as a frightened bride of eighteen. My husband Karl was twenty and I looked to him for everything. A quiet man, but such strength in that quietness. How I depended on him! Too much, really. That is why I nearly went crazy when I found myself unable to call upon that strength.

In those days it was not so easy to leave home and family to cross an ocean. But since we were young and full of high spirits, it all seemed a great adventure. Being short of money, we embarked from Gothenburg on a cargo boat that carried passengers. The ocean was rough … waves high as hillsides … and I discovered that I was not a good sailor. How that ship would *rulla* and *stampa*. Those are Swedish words for roll and pitch. And that's exactly what that boat did. I was seasick the whole time.

Karl was my Rock of Gibraltar. I do not believe I could have survived without him. When at last we disembarked, I was so glad to be ashore I kneeled down to kiss the dock. I was more than a little afraid, though, not knowing any English and weak from the long trip. But Karl soon found us a place to stay. Not a palace, to be sure, only a small room in a low-priced hotel. But I welcomed any bed, so long as it was on solid ground.

Fall was coming on, and the room was cold. It didn't bother me too much — I was a farm girl raised in the northern part of Sweden. But Karl, coming from the southwest coast, suffered terribly. When morning came, he left me alone and set out to find work.

It's strange, is it not, how little things in life can mean so very much. Little things … little kindnesses. Once they happen, they are never forgotten.

Karl was out looking for any kind of employment every day that week. When he came home empty-handed on Friday night, his face was grey and drawn. We went out to a diner for hamburgers, washing them down with the worst coffee I had ever tasted.

That evening I noticed Karl was breathing with great difficulty. At first I thought he was just tired from the long search for a job. But he got worse. 'Ingrid, Ingrid,' he called out to me during the night. I knew it to be a cry for help. I did not know what to do, which way to turn. There I was, alone in a strange land with no knowledge of English. Karl had never been ill before. Towards morning, he became hot and feverish. I knew I had to get a doctor right away.

The clerk at the desk downstairs just looked at me and scratched his head when I tried to make him understand. Finally, I clutched his arm and refused to let go, all the while trying to drag him to the elevator. At length, he came with me to the room. As soon as he saw Karl, he returned to his desk and called for a doctor.

A short time later, a silver-haired man with a black bag came into our room. He examined Karl and shook his head. He said the word 'emergency'. I didn't know for sure what it meant, but it had an awful sound.

I was crying when the ambulance arrived. The attendants couldn't understand me when I tried to ask them questions, but they let me ride with Karl to the hospital. It was a cold morning. Freezing rain was falling.

In the hospital waiting room, they left me sitting on a black leather chair and wheeled my husband away between swinging doors. I watched those doors for a long time. I began to fear that I would never see my Karl again.

It was then, when I felt myself beyond hope, that she approached me. A tiny figure, all robed in black and white, like a little bird. She had the gentlest brown eyes. Taking my hand in hers, she spoke several English words, slowly and distinctly — as though her determination alone could make me understand. I shook my head. '*Parlez vous francaise?*' she enquired. Again, I shook my head. '*Verstehen sie deutch?*'

After that she tried Italian. Her supply of languages seemed inexhaustible — as well as her patience. But I was growing more panicky by the moment.

'*Jag tolar svenska*,' I cried. '*Svenska!*'

It was her turn to shake her head. I have often wondered where she got the idea to do what she did then. The good Sister squeezed my hand and disappeared as quickly as she had arrived. I was more miserable than ever. But a short time later she returned. She was holding out a strawberry ice-cream cone. When she smiled and gave it to me, I knew everything was going to be all right. After all, one is not expected to eat ice-cream if one's husband is seriously ill. *'Tack, Sister,'* I cried. *'Tack, tack.'* In my heart, I thank her still.

As it turned out, Karl had only a bad case of pleurisy. He was out of that hospital in a couple of days. And he is still with me today. Stand up, Karl, so everyone can see you.

This country has been good to us. We have three grandchildren and two great-grandchildren. And we are all partial to strawberry ice-cream!"

Saturation Point

Although Hal had been drinking heavily all day, he was feeling relatively sober when he set out for the Odeon at six-thirty. A new horror flick was playing and he didn't want to wait for the second show at nine. There was always a line up for it. He hated lining up for anything.

That was one of the many issues he and Ruth Anne had invariably disagreed over, Hal reflected, as he parked his car and turned up the collar of his leather jacket against a biting March wind. Ruth Anne had always complained about getting ready early enough to be at the theatre by seven. And she never wanted to see the same films he did. She liked gushy sentimental slop. He was well rid of her, he decided. Women were more damn trouble than they were worth. He'd had half a dozen steadies since he'd left school, and none of them had panned out. He'd be better off settling for one-night stands. Picking up chicks was never a problem; they all seemed to go for his lean body and dark good looks. Hell, all he had to do was whistle …

He flicked his cigarette butt away and went inside to the ticket seller, a heavily made-up brunette of indeterminate age who always reminded him of his mother. My mother the actress, waiting on tables in Toronto restaurants between acting jobs. She should be able to find roles easily, he thought wryly. She was a damn good actress. Once or twice she'd even managed to convince Hal she cared about him.

"One, please," he said.

One, please. Could have been his mother's order for children. Well, good thing she stopped when she did in view of the fact his old man had jumped ship when Hal was only five. Several years earlier, when Hal was an idealistic nineteen, he had managed to track down his father through several relatives on that side of the family. They had met briefly in Winnipeg, facing each other in the lobby of a seedy hotel, two strangers with nothing but a surname in common. Hal had expected to feel something — even anger would have been preferable to the indifference that caused him to cut their reunion short. A couple of years later, he heard that the old man had died of cancer.

In spite of its eye-catching title, Hal found *Let Me Kill You Sweetheart* providing very little in the way of entertainment. It wasn't as good as some of the video games he'd had as a seven-year-old kid. There'd been one decently realistic scene of a female body suspended from a meat hook, but it hadn't exactly made him sit up and take notice. In another part, a severed head had been squashed like a melon, but somehow the blood didn't look real. Hal was actually becoming bored with the whole thing when he grew aware of a figure slipping into the seat next to him. He caught a whiff of Ruth Anne's lily-of-the-valley perfume.

"It's me, Hal," she whispered.

"How come they let you in halfway through the film?"

"I bribed them. Hal, could we go somewhere and talk?"

"There's nothing to talk about, Ruth Anne."

"How can you say that?"

"Easy. It's true."

The man in front of them turned around. "Go home if you wanna talk," he growled.

For a few minutes they sat quietly, watching the film. Brandishing a meat cleaver, the psychopathic killer was stalking his ex-wife in a deserted warehouse. The background music sounded familiar, but Hal couldn't quite place it. He could feel Ruth Anne staring at him in the darkness.

"Please, Hal," she whispered.

"It's over between us. Can't you get that through your head?"

The man in the seat ahead of them got up and moved to one several rows away.

"We had something going for us, Hal. Just because we had one little fight …"

"It wasn't the fight, Ruth Anne. I just … well, our sack time got to be so boring …"

He heard the sharp intake of breath and turned to glance at her. She had tears in her eyes. Curious, he thought, how they shone in the faint light from the movie screen. The tear in her left eye looked ready to fall, yet it remained suspended. Then the action in the film took a new twist, and Hal barely noticed Ruth Anne's departure.

The psycho had cornered his ex and was hacking at her breasts, cleaver dripping with blood. This was more like it. Real excitement. Looked absolutely authentic. Even the blood. Only maybe the scene was going on a bit too long.

Losing its shock value. Director's fault. He should have known when to quit. Hitchcock always knew. Hal recalled seeing *Psycho* on TV when he was about seven years old. Now that had been a shocker. He used to see lots of good stuff like that on television when he was a kid. Especially when his old lady was working nights.

At nine o'clock Hal filed out along with the sparse number of early theatre goers. As always, there was a long line of half-frozen people coming in for the second show. He glanced at their faces as he left, but he didn't see anyone he knew. He figured if he did, he'd tell them to save their money, that the title was the only good thing about this flick.

The drinks he'd had earlier had worn off completely, and Hal felt a raging thirst. He decided to leave his car where it was and walk to the nearest bar. The wind had gone down and there was a full moon. It was a good night for walking.

The first beer hit the spot, and he ordered another. By the time he'd tossed back half a dozen, the skinny little female singer in the rock group was beginning to look pretty good. He went up to her at the end of the last set. "Buy you a drink?" he asked.

She studied him up and down, brown eyes coolly appraising. "Thanks, but I'm really beat tonight. We were on the road at eight o'clock this morning. Can I take a rain check?"

When he made no reply, she went on. "How about tomorrow night?"

"Why not," he agreed. "I could use some sack time myself." He started to walk away but turned back. "What's your name?"

"Donna," she replied.

"Okay, Donna. See you tomorrow night."

Feeling pleased with himself, Hal headed for the washroom. He didn't like the idea of the long walk back to his car, but there was nothing he could do about that now.

The night was still clear, but the wind had risen again. He thought about Donna's compact little body as he walked. He might come back tomorrow and then again he might not. At least this chick would be on her way in a week's time. He probably would come back, he decided. Good a way as any to spend his last free night. He always hated going back to work after his days off. Being a process operator was such a dull job. Looking at dials for eight hours. He'd only chosen it because the salary was better than for most jobs. Manpower had paid him to go to college to take the course. They hadn't paid him very damn much though.

Barely enough to live on. His sports car was the first thing he'd bought when …

Hal's thoughts were interrupted as he turned the corner. A distraught woman ran forward and tried to grab his arm. "Come help us!" she cried. "Please! Two young punks are beating on my husband, trying to rob us …"

Hal pulled away from her, repelled by her puffy face and dyed red hair. The three males were struggling beside a blue car by the curb a few yards from where his own car was parked. The old geezer, the woman's husband, no doubt, went down on his knees while Hal watched.

Screaming, the woman flew at her man's assailants. She moved pretty fast for an old fatso, Hal thought. One of the teenagers was trying to wrestle her handbag from her, but she was putting up quite a fight. "For the love of God!" she cried out to Hal, "Give me a hand!"

Slowly, Hal raised his hands. He clapped resoundingly half a dozen times. Then he hurried to his car and got into it without looking back.

Meg Would Love To See You

"Lana! What a surprise! It is you, isn't it?"

Halted in my headlong rush down Cromwell Street. A familiar face. One half of that couple who used to live on the third floor across from us. Dennis the Dentist. Or almost. Probably has a few months to go before graduating. His wife the breadwinner. On her feet clerking all day in a department store.

"Small world," I mumble. "How long has it been?"

"Since we left Mrs. Mulvaney's madhouse? About two years. You still there, Lana?"

"Yep. Cheap rent. And I don't have to pay entertainment tax."

His laugh is boyish still, making him even more attractive. "I can hear our old landlady now," he says, "singing the top forty on her feudal rounds. Hey — come have coffee, Lana. Our digs are nearby. Meg would love to see you. She has Thursdays off."

"Well … I do have a couple of hours."

"Say no more. Be like old times. You still living with that fellow … what's his name?"

"Bill. Sweet William. No, he went back up north."

"Sorry."

"I'm not. We were arguing about everything. When we couldn't even agree on the weather, we knew it was time to call it quits."

The front of his apartment building is drab, but the inside is a revelation.

"Is this how struggling students live?" I ask, taking in the Swedish modern décor.

"Meg gets a good discount on everything in the store. And you know her. House proud. Keeps everything spotless."

"Speaking of Meg, where is she?"

"She's around somewhere. Sit down. I'll be right back."

He returns with tall glasses on a tray, ice clinking seductively. Tom Collins. Cool drinks on a hot day. I'm getting wary but can't resist a sip.

When he slides a disk into the machine in the corner, Sinatra's mellow tones issue forth. I'm no longer wary. I'm convinced. And I'm outraged. So Meg's working all these years for this creep. How to get even? An answer comes right after the question. But first I have to get rid of Dennis for a minute.

"Got any cheese?" I ask. "I really shouldn't drink on an empty stomach."

A rat should be able to find cheese fast, I reflect, going into action the minute he leaves the room.

I'm ready for his return. "It isn't Meg's day off, is it, Dennis? I'm getting out of here. Don't try to stop me."

He shrugs. "I'm not into violence. Just looking for a little diversion."

It's still hot outside, but the air seems fresh compared to what I've left. Good old Dennis the Dentist. He'll have a little diversion, all right. He'll have a little trouble explaining the pink silk panties I slid beneath the sofa cushions. Expensive ones, too. But we women have to stick together.

The Night Visitor

Anna Martinelli returned to consciousness slowly, as though loath to leave the illusions of night for whatever realities the day might bring. She kept her ears pillow-closed against the singing of the city birds, her eyes tightly shut against the brightness of the morning sun. But both birds and sun persisted until the old lady opened her faded eyes and grudgingly recognized the beginning of another day.

Carmen, her youngest grandchild, entered with a breakfast tray. "Nonna," she asked, "did he come again last night?"

The old lady managed a smile. Nonna for Grandma. Even though her daughter had married a fifth generation Canadian, traces of the old country still remained. They remained in the child too, in her searching brown eyes, her raven's wing of black hair, the music in her voice.

"Did he come, Nonna?" the child repeated, setting the tray on the bedside table. "Did your Night Visitor come?"

Anna supported herself on a shaking elbow to take a sip of strong hot coffee. "Si, Carmenita, he came."

"Did he have the dog with him?"

"You know your momma doesn't like me filling your head with these wild stories, as she calls them."

The little girl climbed up to perch on the edge of the bed, smoothing her bright blue cotton dress around her. "Tell me again what he looks like."

Anna took another sip of coffee. She began slowly, but her voice gathered momentum as she went on. "Well, he's very tall, very straight, and his hair is shining silver. He wears a black suit and a black tie, but his shirt is white. So white it seems to glow. There's a white flower in his buttonhole. He has dark eyes that seem to see everything, and the kindest, warmest smile you could ever imagine. Oh, and he has a big silver mustache and a dimple in his chin."

Carmen leaned forward eagerly. "And the dog, Nonna. Does he still have the dog with him?"

"Si, si, the dog is always close to him. It, too, has a kind face. A big, silvery-colored police dog. A beautiful dog."

"Does the man ever touch you?"

"No, but each night he comes a little nearer. Like last night. He reached out his hand towards me."

"He did!" Carmen jumped down from the bed. "It's so exciting, Nonna. I wish I had a Night Visitor like you."

The old woman smiled thinly. "Perhaps some day you will have. When you're as old as I am."

Wordlessly, they regarded each other across the abyss of years.

"Did he scare you?" the child asked suddenly. "The first time he came, I mean."

"No, dear. He was so far away I could barely see him. But each night, he moves a little nearer. Now he sits beside me on the bed. And the dog lies at his feet."

"I have to go now," said Carmen, picking up the breakfast tray. "But I'll come up to see you when I get back from the pool. I can do a real dive now. And swim four whole lengths! Oh, Nonna, I wish the summer would last forever!"

"Nothing lasts forever, child. Not in this world." With that, she sank back against her pillows. "Run along now. Do a swan dive for me."

For Anna Martinelli, the long August day passed as slowly, as uneventfully as had all the days since she'd been bedridden. Almost a year now. A year of waiting, interspersed with dutiful visits from her daughter, son-in-law and older grandchildren. That was understandable, she decided. They were involved with the living of life, she with the leaving of it.

Well, she had lived more than her three score and ten. Poor Gino had been granted so much less. She had lost him in a construction accident early in their marriage — when their only child, a girl, was younger even than Carmen. Anna lived with that daughter now. Their roles had been irrevocably reversed.

There had been a time, Anna remembered, when she had seriously considered the idea of marrying again, primarily so her daughter would have a father to see her through the growing years. But her belief in an afterlife was strong, and the thought of having it cluttered up with two husbands did not appeal to her. Besides, it would have been unfair. She had loved Gino so very much no one could ever really have taken his place.

Anna closed her eyes, recalling her wedding day. She was back in Naples again, the sun warm on her young cheeks, Gino's kiss of betrothal warmer still. Fifty-eight years ago. Fifty-eight years, and she could remember still the taste of the wine, the joy of their wedding feast, Gino beside her, straight and tall, his dark good looks, his strength, the feel of his arms around her.

Anna twisted about, trying to find a comfortable position. How small her body felt now! How insubstantial. For a few minutes, she listened to the usual noises of the bustling household below. Then she slipped back into time.

Raising a strong-willed daughter in a new country had not been easy for her. The girl constantly accused her of being old country, old-fashioned. Every time she protested some new teenage tribal rite, she was met with fiery opposition. It was with a great deal of relief she saw her daughter through school and safely married. Then, for the first time, Anna was able to think about herself.

The job she'd held for years in a dry-cleaning store was not enough of a challenge for her. She'd decided to get out before she became as dull and dispirited as the middle-aged manager — a woman who looked as though she herself had been dry-cleaned, emerging with every frown line and wrinkle intact. Anna wanted to live again — to get out into the big exciting world of her adopted country, to meet the city on its own terms — and win. She took a business course in night school, moved from that to a real-estate office, and, at a time when such an occupation was rare for a woman, became finally a real-estate saleswoman. Many of her countrymen were coming over, and she was extremely successful in her new career. So successful she went on working long after the usual retirement age. She'd maintained her own apartment plus a cheerful independence until, shortly after her seventy-seventh birthday, illness struck. Then long months in the hospital, long months here in her daughter's home with only her memories to sustain her. And she had had enough of remembering.

Anna reached for the bell on her bedside table. How terrible it was to be helpless after so active a life! She found herself praying for night to draw a curtain of permanent release.

At last another interminable day was over. Wearing a long cotton gown, Carmen padded into her room on small bare feet.

"Aren't you supposed to be in bed?" Anna whispered.

"Tell me more about your Night Visitor. Please, Nonna?"

"Promise you'll go right to bed if I do."

"I promise."

Anna fell asleep as soon as she finished talking. The child tip-toed from her room, closing the door softly behind her.

Early the next morning, Carmen's mother entered her daughter's room. Tearfully, she began to try to explain why it had been necessary for her nonna to go away.

"I know why," interrupted the girl, her manner untroubled. "Last night the Night Visitor took her hand. He took her away with him."

"Carmen, I will not have you repeating those wild stories." The plump, dark-haired woman sat down on her child's bed and started leafing idly through the Bible she'd taken from the drawer of her mother's bedside table. As she did so, an old photograph fluttered down to land face-up on the quilted yellow spread before them.

Carmen leaned forward to study it. "That looks just like him!" she cried, picking up the picture. "See, Momma! He's even got the dog with him. Only it's darker looking here. And the man's got dark hair too, and a black mustache. Nonna said it was silver. But it's the same man. He's even got the white flower in his coat. And a dimple in his chin. See!"

Carmen's mother reached for the photo. "Honey, don't you know who this is? It's your grandfather Gino, taken on his wedding day."

"But he's the one, Momma. He's the Night Visitor. Honest!"

Long moments passed in unbroken silence before mother and daughter gradually became aware of the insistent singing of the city birds.

The Winter Of Netta Cooper's Discontent

Netta Cooper's first glimpse of Derek Robinson should have sent her running from the meeting of the St. Paul Women's Guild. She suspected she was going through some sort of change-of-life crisis. Her husband Keith was doing more than his usual amount of travelling. Even when he was home, he was always so tired he'd fall asleep the minute his head hit the pillow. He hadn't even noticed the sexy silk nightgown she'd bought. She'd spent an hour finding one that matched the exact shade of her green eyes, her best feature. She'd put on a CD of their favourite love songs. Nothing seemed to interest Keith, to rekindle the passion he once felt for her. Not that she expected miracles. After all, they'd been married for twenty years. She knew he was putting in long hours at work, and he was doing it for her and the children. But surely there should be some spark of the feelings they'd once shared. Lately it seemed as though their lives consisted only of working, paying bills, and driving the kids to their various activities.

Netta couldn't deny it. As soon as her eyes had caught Derek Robinson's it was a case of lust at first sight. He fitted exactly her idea of how an artist should look. Bohemian. Slightly dangerous, very exotic. The way he'd smiled at her. She couldn't stop picturing that smile.

At that meeting, the women of the Guild had decided Netta should be the one to make the arrangements for their commissioned painting — a mural for the newly decorated basement room of the church. She should have refused.

The whole affair had a preposterous flavour. St. Paul of all saints! St. Paul to whom the words sex and sin were practically synonymous.

* * *

Now the time has come to face him. Netta takes a deep breath and rings the doorbell. She fears her feelings will be humiliatingly obvious. *Stop this*, she tells herself. *You have a good husband and three great kids. You chose to be a stay-at-home mother. You have no business letting your imagination run wild.*

Netta forgets her fears when she and Derek begin to talk. They fall into a sort of mystical rapport almost at once. She's glad she's worn her moss green dress. She knows it brings out the colour in her eyes. She could be a *cougar*, too, she thinks, like those high-powered career women who go after younger men. She's just read an article about them in one of the magazines she subscribes to.

After Derek shows her around his studio, she pauses for long moments to study a carved wooden crucifix — old as the suffering of humankind, new as a space age missile.

"Do you like it?" he asks, his deep voice seeming to surround her. "I did that piece last year. It's one I'm particularly fond of — though I know that sounds like bragging."

"It's beautiful."

"So are you. The sunlight has set your hair on fire, like the biblical burning bush." He chuckles. "No pun intended."

Smiling, Netta turns to him. He, too, is beautiful, dappled with red, yellow, and blue light coming through the stained-glass window high above them. Like a Renaissance painting. "Did you design that window?"

"Yes. I think now I must have done so for you to stand in its reflected light."

"Mr. Robinson," she begins.

"Please. Just Derek."

"About this mural for our church …"

He glances at his watch. "Time for my coffee break. *Creme de cafie*," he adds, smiling. I usually have a liqueur this time of the afternoon. Won't you join me? We can talk business over a drink."

"It wouldn't be proper," Netta replies.

"Slave to propriety, are we?" he teases, his blue eyes amused, slightly mocking.

"Not at all. I make my own decisions."

"Then join me. Let's make it *creme de menthe*. There's a touch of spring in the air."

He takes a bottle from his liquor cabinet, pours a small amount of the pale green liquid into two crystal glasses, and leads the way to a black leather sofa at the far end of the room.

A sudden weakness in Netta's knees forces her to sit down.

"A paler version of your lovely eyes," he says.

This is ridiculous, Netta tells herself. *I'm blushing like a schoolgirl, and he's amused.*

Damn him anyway, standing there in his slim chino pants and vee-neck sweater, knowing he's handsome, knowing the sweater's the exact blue of his eyes with their impossibly long black lashes. "I haven't much time," she says brusquely.

"We have this moment, Netta. Let's live it to the full."

"My husband will soon be home," she lies, knowing Keith will be in Edmonton till the end of the week. "I'd better go."

Gently, Derek places the glass in her hand. "One drink," he says, "to our upcoming transaction — and mutual satisfaction."

Netta sips nervously as he sinks down beside her, resting one arm on the back of the sofa. Her heart is beating much too fast. If only she could turn the tables on Derek Robinson, make *him* feel uncomfortable …

His kiss catches her completely by surprise. But she's trembling less with anger than with the excitement of feeling his lips on hers. His beard and moustache are silky soft. She's never before kissed a man with a beard. It's a decidedly pleasant experience.

"I'm not going to say I'm sorry," he murmurs, leaning back and tracing the curve of her cheek with his thumb, "because I'm not. You feel the same, don't you, Netta. Why deny it? We knew this would happen from the first time our eyes met at the meeting in St. Paul's. I couldn't stop staring at you. Such instant attraction is a rare and valuable gift — one we shouldn't just throw away."

She rises unsteadily to her feet. "I'm a married woman," she protests. "I have three children. Besides, I'm years older than you."

"Age means nothing to me. As for your husband, I don't see why love has to be rationed. Strict marital fidelity only made sense when men might be saddled with raising offspring not their own."

"Derek, I was married at nineteen. I've never known any man, in the biblical sense, other than my husband."

"Don't you think it's time you did?"

Netta can't help herself. Part of her agrees with him. She had met Mr. Right far too early in her life. She is curious about other men. Surely it will do no harm to …

"You won't have to worry that I'll make trouble for you or bother you in any way. I'm not that kind of man." He speaks as though he has been reading her thoughts.

"What kind are you? The kind who tries to make love to every woman he meets?"

"Far from it. I'm often lonely. But I'd rather be lonely than be with someone I don't care for." He reaches out to take her hand in his. "I could care for you, Netta. I haven't felt this way about anyone for a long time."

She glances down at their empty glasses standing side by side, almost touching. "This could cause only heartbreak," she says. "We both know that, Derek."

"Only if we let it. I know you have a husband and family. I know they'll always come first with you. We're not a couple of teenagers. Believe me, Netta, we'll harm no one. We'll simply enrich each other's life. I haven't been with anyone for a long time. Too long."

"Derek, I have to go."

"Not yet. Please. Besides, we haven't even talked about the mural."

"I'll have one of the other women come to see you tomorrow." She smiles tentatively. "I don't trust myself around you."

"No. You come. I'll be waiting."

Netta remains silent while he helps her on with her coat. At the doorway, she turns, committing his face to memory, determined that she will not see him again.

* * *

When she reaches her split-level home in the suburbs, Netta parks her brown station wagon in the driveway and heads for the safety of her front door, wishing she could open it and find Keith there. The emptiness of the house is unbearable. Moving like a robot she starts dinner for the boys and Lisa. She takes chicken breasts from the freezer and puts them in the microwave to thaw. Then she begins to peel potatoes and carrots.

When they arrive home, the children rattle on about their day, seemingly unaware of her preoccupation. Why should they be? she asks herself. As long as I'm here doing the same old job. Dependable old mom. Just someone to do the cooking, laundry and cleaning. And what of Keith? Business trips weren't always all business. Maybe Keith was having a little adventure of his own right now. What harm would it do if she were to see Derek again? Just a little flirtation. She wouldn't let it go too far. She couldn't be untrue to Keith. Away from home or not, she feels in her heart that he has always been faithful to her. They'd had five glorious carefree years together before starting a family. What fun he'd been in those days! He seemed so different now. So settled in his ways. So serious. She craves adventure. Excitement. She will soon be forty years old. A person's life shouldn't be over at thirty-nine, she thinks. She spends the rest of her day in a daze, changing her mind a dozen times about whether or not to see Derek again.

After a restless night, Netta moves trance-like through the hectic routine of getting the children off to catch their school buses. As she sits down with her second cup of coffee, the telephone rings. It's Keith, sounding troubled.

"Something's come up," he says. "I'm going to have to fly out to the coast. Be gone another week at least."

"Oh, Keith, no!"

"Sorry, Netta. Can't be helped."

"No, I guess not." While they talk of other matters, her mind is in turmoil. She's relieved when at last she's able to replace the receiver. The kitchen is quiet again, so quiet she can hear the ticking of the clock. Time is passing her by. Life is passing her by.

At one o'clock the next day, a nervous Netta is pressing the buzzer at Derek's studio, the collar of her spring coat turned up, her eyes hidden by dark glasses.

"Come in, Mata Hari," he says, laughing.

And everything is all right again. Netta removes her sunglasses, takes his hand, and walks with him through the rays of coloured light streaming through the stained-glass window.

Two hours later she is dabbing at her eyes and trying hard to act her age. Derek puts one arm around her shoulders and strokes her hair with the other. "Netta, don't. Relax now. Everything will be all right. How about a little *creme de cacao?*"

"Please."

The sweet liquid warms her, but it's Derek's gentleness, his quiet words against her ear that finally take the chill from her.

Netta is late arriving home. Before she can duck inside, her neighbour, Flo Williams, plump but not pleasant, collars her. "Got time for a coffee and the latest?"

The two women sit in Netta's colonial-style kitchen facing each other over steaming mugs. "I'd better tell you this before your boys get home," says Flo, "not that they probably haven't already heard. After all, they go to the same school as that Denning girl. Maybe they're even involved. Sometimes I'm glad that I was never blessed with children. That Denning girl always acted so sweet, too, not like the ones that wear their skirts up to God knows where. Just goes to show you."

"Flo, I'm running late today. Just what is it you're trying to say?"

"Well, it seems Virginia Denning has been sleeping with every boy in Grade Nine." Flo pauses to reach for her fourth chocolate chip cookie. "Imagine! The little tramp."

As her neighbour's shrill voice goes on and on, Netta finds herself irritated by the constantly moving jaws, the malicious gossip. She wants desperately to be alone with her thoughts. Will she go back again? No, definitely not. Well, maybe just once ... just to explain why she won't see him again ... he'd been so sweet to her, afterwards ...

"Netta, are you listening? You look like you're a hundred miles away."

Only about five, Netta thinks. But the distance is infinite. Her world is here, with Keith and the children. No, she will not go back. Definitely not. "I'm sorry, Flo. I must have spring fever or something."

"It's still February. Still lots of winter ahead."

My winter of discontent, Netta thinks as she sees her neighbour to the door, feeling a strong urge to push her through it.

* * *

Netta goes back to Derek Robinson's studio not once, but twice, before she can bring herself to finally say goodbye. By that time, it's much easier to end the affair than she had expected. True, she's suffered a great deal of remorse over breaking the sixth commandment, but her real reason for ending it is a much more basic one. Her curiosity has been satisfied. Making love with Derek hadn't been so very different from making love with Keith. Except that with Keith it had always seemed so right, so natural.

Derek protests, his blue eyes filled with pain that surprises her. She hadn't taken his feelings into account at all. She had been completely selfish, she sees that now.

"Netta, don't leave me so soon. We're just getting to know each other. I care for you — more than you know. More than I should."

"I have to, Derek. I'm sorry."

"We haven't decided about the mural for St. Paul's yet."

"You'll think of something suitable, I have trust in your judgment."

"All I can think of is The Song of Solomon. 'Behold thou art fair, my love ...'"

"Maybe you should do the woman being stoned for adultery."

"Netta, don't. There are few today who would dare cast the first stone."

"I have to go now."

"Not yet. Please."

There's a strange catch in his voice, and she puts her arms around him. "I'm truly sorry, Derek. I just can't manage this emotionally. I feel so guilty …" She bursts into tears and turns away from him.

He walks beside her to the door. "Don't ever be sorry. And don't feel guilty. It was mostly my fault, what happened. And, Netta, I'll do a beautiful mural for you. I'll do Ruth gleaning barley in the fields. I'll do Ruth washed in sunshine. And I'll be thinking of you with every brush stroke."

"Good-bye, Derek," she murmurs. "I'll never forget you."

* * *

Keith returns home the following Saturday morning, his face wreathed in smiles, his suitcase bulging with surprises. For a long time, Netta holds him close. How good it is to have him back. Balding head, slight paunch and all.

"It sure is good to be home, honey. I missed you and the kids."

She looks into his warm brown eyes and feels a small sadness stir within her.

Lisa comes into the room and he scoops their daughter into a warm bear hug. She's followed by the boys, all blue jeans, sweat shirts, and broad smiles. "How was the trip, Dad?"

"A smashing success. How come you guys aren't over at Hal's practising for the big game?"

"Hal's grounded for a whole month. Serves him right, too. Virginia Denning wouldn't promise to go to the school dance with him so he spread some rotten lies about her. Everybody was talking about her, making fun of her first name. His mother got everything sorted out fast."

Netta recalls her neighbour's gossip and it leaves her feeling slightly sick. She hopes Hal has learned his lesson. What a cruel thing for the boy to do. Making an innocent girl suffer like that. "Look what I have for you, honey," her husband is saying. He holds out a silk robe — fields of daisies on clouds of blue. "Daisies won't tell," he teases.

Netta swallows hard and buries her face against the roughness of his tweed suit coat. Was everything to be a double entendre to her now? How she wishes she could turn back the clock.

Somehow, Netta manages to get through the day. That night, in Keith's arms, she tries to cancel out the past. She feels safe in his arms, protected. "I hope you won't have to go away again too soon," she says. "I miss you so. I hate being alone."

Next morning, after church, Lisa and the boys climb into the back seat of the station wagon and they set out on one of their leisurely Sunday drives, drives that have always been her favourite part of the day. But the sense of family solidarity eludes her. Frightened, she stares at her husband's strong, aquiline profile. She knows him well enough to know that, if called upon, he would bear the burden of her guilt. He'd had a few relationships before they married. He might understand and forgive her. It would make her feel better to tell him, to confess everything. Maybe later tonight.

"Who wants to stop for a milkshake?" he asks. "Don't all answer at once."

His familiar question touches Netta. He's such a basically good man. It isn't his fault he has to be away on business so often. No, she will never inflict the burden of her guilt on him. Her winter of discontent will not be made glorious summer.

The small sadness creeps back to take up residence somewhere deep inside her. It will, she believes, take a long time to go away.

Saint Nicholas Corrigan

It was going to be a very special Christmas — the last one the Corrigans would spend together as a family of five. The gifts, Nicholas decided, would have to be as special as the occasion. He'd been saving every cent he could from his after school job at the supermarket. He had a fat wallet. He waved it in front of his mother on Saturday morning.

"Are you sure you don't want my help, Nick?" she asked. "Christmas shopping isn't easy."

"Thanks but no thanks, Mom. I know you guys better than you know yourselves."

With that, he was off. He thought about his family as he rode downtown on the bus. His older sisters would soon be leaving home — Marnie was getting married and Rita would be going away to university to major in business administration. His big sisters. Both so different, but each holding a large claim on his affections. He would miss them.

Gift shopping for his family was always easy. He knew them all so well. His mom, pretty, but down-to-earth and practical. His dad, a bit of a dreamer. Marnie took after him. She lived in a make-believe world of glamour. Rita, with her short black hair and glasses, was a whiz at business. For her, he would have to find something useful. Nothing like those red satin pyjamas on a mannequin across the aisle from him. But they'd be perfect for Marnie. Match her lips and nails. Rita didn't even wear make-up.

The pyjamas took quite a bite out of his shopping money, but he had enough to buy a pocket calculator for Rita, an art book of Van Gogh's work for his father, and a popcorn maker for his mother. Pleased with his purchases, he could hardly wait for Christmas morning, just two days away.

"Mom!" he shouted when he got home, "where's the gift wrap?"

Marnie was standing beside the Christmas tree. "Remember this one, Nick?" she asked, flipping back her long, blonde hair as she pointed to a white egg suspended from a red velvet ribbon on the pine branch above her head.

Nick looked at the decoration. It had a hand-painted picture of their house on it, perfect right down to the red roses by the front door, done by a local artist.

"I sure do. I used to think it was a real egg shell when I was little. I always worried about dropping it. You guys might have told me it was plastic."

His sister laughed. "And spoil all the fun? Never."

His mother handed him a roll of gold coloured paper. "Hurry and wrap your gifts. We're invited next door for eggnog. Your dad and Rita have left already."

* * *

Christmas morning brought with it a fresh fall of snow. It blanketed the evergreens outside the Corrigans' picture window making everything postcard-perfect. Like an old-fashioned Yuletide greeting card, Nick reflected. "Open my gifts first," he urged his family."

Rita picked up an oblong box covered in gold wrap. "This one has my name on it," she announced, so I'll start."

With a sick feeling, Nick realized that he had somehow switched the names on his sisters' gifts. He started to explain, but he was too late. Rita was pulling out the red pyjamas with an expression of pure delight. "Wow! I've always wanted to wear something like this!" she cried.

Seconds later, Nick found himself in a perfumed hug from Marnie. "How did you ever guess I wanted a calculator? You must have read my mind. Thanks, bro. You're the greatest."

With sudden inspiration, Nick scooped up his parents' presents and removed the tags. He gave one to his mother.

"I don't believe it!" she exclaimed. "I was looking at this very art book a few weeks ago, but I decided it was too expensive. Thank you, Nick."

His dad was equally pleased. "I've always wanted to try my hand at making cheese popcorn," he said. "I can't wait to try it. You are one great shopper, son."

Nicholas grinned hugely. Maybe someday he'd tell them. Someday years and years from now. "Ho, ho, ho," he boomed. "Merry Christmas, everybody!"

Seventh Day Of May

Thank heavens for daughters, Lorna Langtry reflected as Eloise drove her to the hospital on the morning of her scheduled operation. Her son Jeff couldn't understand her refusal to tell Frank Wilkins, but Eloise had nodded with complete understanding.

"It's just that he's so *athletic*," Lorna had explained. "If he knows I'm getting a hip replacement, he won't look at me the same way."

She'd very nearly chickened out of the whole thing at the pre-op clinic a week earlier. Seeing the cast showing a titanium ball and socket had been bad enough, but all the "don'ts" worried her even more. Don't bend your new hip more than ninety degrees, don't cross your legs, don't turn your operated leg inward. She'd have to rent a walker and a high toilet seat. She'd have to buy a reacher — a device for picking things up off the floor — for the first six weeks. It was all so complicated.

"I wouldn't be doing this if I could still walk," she said. "Those darned anti-inflammatory pills just wouldn't work any more. I hope you never get osteoarthritis, Eloise."

"I hope not, Mom. I sympathize, I really do."

The streets were practically deserted in the mists of early dawn. It would be a lovely last day of April morning. But not for her. Still, she'd come this far. There was no backing out now. She'd made two blood donations for her own use at the Red Cross clinic in London, sixty miles away. She'd seen the internist who'd given her an ultrasound, an ECG, then pronounced, smiling, "You'll come through the operation just fine."

So why did she feel she was sitting on Death Row, rather than in Eloise's little Ford Escort? You're a coward, that's why, she told herself. A sniveling, spineless coward. A poor role model for Eileen and Irene, her twelve-year-old twin granddaughters.

Maybe she should have told Frank after all. She would have, if he hadn't been going on and on about how glad he was that she was so fit at sixty-five, how they were going to have a great summer, camping in the Pinery, hiking trails there. Up until a short time ago, she'd been able to hide the pain from him. Then she'd concocted a story about having to spend a couple of months with her aging mother in England. He'd bought the fabrication, hook, line, and sinker.

All her friends had been sworn to secrecy. She didn't want Frank finding out from any of them.

"You'd better go," she told Eloise as soon as she was settled in her room. "Soon be time for you to get the girls off to school."

She almost weakened and called Frank when Eloise left. The phone was too handy — right beside her bed. A nurse came in, handed her a blue hospital gown and gave her a black marker.

"What's this for?" Lorna asked.

"Put an X on the leg to be operated on."

"You're kidding! I was making jokes about doing that."

"Can't be too careful," said the nurse as she left her alone once more.

When they wheeled her into the operating room, Lorna's gaze moved apprehensively around the mint-green figures hovering above her. "I have cold feet," she complained. Her mind was playing with the words "literally" and "figuratively" as she went under the anesthetic.

The next morning, the orthopedic surgeon came to see her. "The operation was a success," he assured her.

But the patient died, she added mentally. Indeed, she feared she had little chance of surviving. Her right leg was strapped to a large, triangular form made of Styrofoam — a form they'd shown her earlier which now felt like some sort of torture rack. She seemed to be connected to tubes everywhere. The one supplying blood was stinging the back of her hand, and her throat felt as dry as if she'd swallowed ten pounds of lint. Every time she pressed the self-administering morphine pump, she would fall asleep only to dream she'd not yet had the operation.

Later in the afternoon, the hallucinations and hives arrived at the same time.

"I must be allergic to morphine," she told the nurse who was taking her temperature. "Look at my arms. I can't stand the itch. And horrible faces keep leering at me from the walls."

"We'll give you something else for the pain," the nurse agreed. "This you don't need."

When Eloise with her husband and the twins arrived, they put their flowers and get-well cards on the table beside her. Eileen and Irene had made the watercolor cards. Lorna managed a few words of praise and was rewarded with identical smiles.

Eloise looked worried. "How are you feeling, Mom?"

"As though my right leg's been replaced by a side of frozen beef."

Eric leaned over, kissed her on the forehead, and took the girls to the hospital cafeteria for Cokes.

"Time to call Kevorkian," Lorna mumbled.

"That's not funny, Mom."

"Neither is this, my darling. Neither is this."

Her son Jeff's flowers arrived just as Eloise was leaving. A dozen yellow roses. Eloise set them on her bedside table so she could enjoy them at close range.

"Your brother had better put himself beside those roses by tomorrow," said Lorna.

Day three brought little relief, but she was given ice cubes to suck and they tasted delicious. Jeff arrived with his girlfriend Pam, their arms filled with books, chocolates, and pink carnations.

"Have you been up yet?" they asked, looking young and concerned — and very windblown from their motorcycle ride from London.

"Not much. I'm too weak. They're giving me two more units of blood. My own wasn't enough. My hemoglobin's gone from eighty-six to sixty-seven, whatever that means." Lorna was miserably aware she must look a sight, what with the plastic oxygen tube stuck up her nose, the blood and IV bags suspended above her, and her curly brown hair a matted mess. Frank would be shocked to see her like this. Thank heavens she hadn't weakened and called him. She had to admit, though, a hug from him would have been most welcome. As though reading her thoughts, Jeff and Pam leaned down to enclose her in fleeting, awkward embraces.

When it was time for them to leave, Jeff turned back to say, "I still think you're making a mistake by not telling Frank."

It was hot in the room that night, and Lorna awoke in the small hours with a pounding headache. She promptly threw up the two white pills she was given to ease the pain.

"Get her some applesauce," said the older of the two nurses.

Sounds good, thought Lorna, preparing for the sweet, fresh coldness of the treat. She opened her mouth eagerly when the young nurse returned and swallowed a spoonful of bitter, ground-up pills that tasted horrible.

"That was mean," she groaned. It did help her to get back to sleep, however, a sleep that was blissfully dream free.

When her family doctor dropped by next morning, he found Lorna sitting in a La-Z-Boy, breakfast tray on the table in front of her. "How's your appetite?" he asked.

"Better than this," she replied, indicating the limp white toast, gluey grey oatmeal porridge and lukewarm coffee.

He smiled. "I see what you mean. Never mind. You'll be able to go home in a few days."

Arrangements had been made for visits from the Victorian Order of Nurses and a therapist, but Lorna felt guilty that Eloise would have to give up her entire holiday from the office in order to look after her. If all this hip business hadn't happened, she and Frank might have been planning a holiday right now. Both widowed for a number of years, they'd met at a seniors' card party two years ago and fallen in love in a matter of weeks. "We're behaving like teenagers," she'd joked.

"Like geriatric delinquents," he'd replied. "Wonderful, isn't it!"

That was the right word, Lorna reflected, for full of wonder it was. She'd never expected to have another man in her life, nor he another woman. Best of all, their children approved of the match — his three sons and her Eloise and Jeff. The last time they'd been together, they'd been discussing whose house they should move into after they married. She liked her bungalow in the city, but his split level on the shore of the St. Clair River was tempting. The river traffic presented a fascinating, ever-changing scene, one they often enjoyed together. Still, driving the river road in the winter could be hazardous. "Maybe we should just toss a coin," Frank had suggested.

Now here she was, stuck with an artificial hip, she who'd always despised all things artificial — flowers, sweeteners, fruit, the palm trees by the pool where she and Frank swam every week. But it would be worth it all in two or three months to be able to swim without pain. You should be grateful, she told herself, to live in an age where such technology is available. She began counting her blessings and found she had plenty to count. Nurses, doctors and therapists were taking excellent care of her. Eloise was a daughter to cherish, and Jeff had been calling her every single day. How she'd produced a computer wizard like him was beyond her. She was still a horse and buggy on the Information Highway. She'd have been a Luddite had she lived in England at the time of the Industrial Revolution.

On Day Five, a pert little nurse approached her. "Time for your first real walk, Mrs. Langtry," she said, un-strapping Lorna's leg from its rigid form and wheeling her walker to the side of the bed.

Clenching her teeth, Lorna moved forward, clumping out through the doorway and down along the corridor. It was a treat to see a wider world again, but every step was heavy and hard-won.

"Good work!" exclaimed the nurse. "Now you know you can do it if you ever need the other hip done."

Lorna looked at her in silence. Any reply she might have made would have been obscene. The girl needed a lesson in tact, no doubt about it. Maybe she wasn't a nurse. The way they dressed these days it was hard to tell.

She and Eloise would share a giggle over it later, she thought, just as they'd laughed at the blurb on the magazine announcing *Gzowski's Hip Replacement*. "If he can do it, I can," Lorna had remarked.

Eloise had opened the magazine to find the article was about Avril Benoit, 'hip' replacement for the Canadian morning show host.

On Day Seven, the surgeon brightened the rainy afternoon by telling Lorna she was fit to go home. "Noon tomorrow," he said. "Who's picking you up?"

"My daughter."

"Good. I'll see you in six weeks."

The next day brought a wealth of May sunshine streaming through her window. Lorna needed the nurse's help to get into the white elastic stockings Eloise had brought earlier, but with the aid of her reacher, she was able to pull on her underwear and a pair of wide-legged, floral-printed pants. She topped them with a long-sleeved white blouse.

Noon seemed to take forever to arrive. Lorna had been given the necessary papers, the wheelchair was waiting, and she'd packed her few belongings in a blue duffel bag. She sat on the edge of her bed, watching the doorway.

When Frank Wilkins appeared to fill that doorway, her mind, for long seconds, refused to recognize his presence.

"Eloise has been keeping me posted all along," he said quietly. "Lorna, how could you keep this from me?"

"How could I tell you?" she replied. "I didn't want you to see me like this. I wanted to wait till I was better. Look at me. I look terrible."

"Yes, you do. You're as white as that blouse you're wearing, and your hair looks like a bird's nest. But, Lorna, I love you."

"I think I was afraid of losing you."

"Love is not love that alters, when it alteration finds. I can't remember where that line comes from, but I believe it."

"Those are just some of Shakespeare's words, Frank. Theory. I can't dress myself. I can't even bend over."

"I'll bend over backwards for you, Lorna. You should have known that. Eloise gave me your house key. I've filled the fridge with goodies. I picked up the special equipment you need from the Red Cross. I even bought you a new La-Z-Boy. You can sit in it to watch your favorite shows. You didn't have one really comfortable chair in your house. I'm going to move in and be your nurse for as long as it takes to get you walking again. I hope you won't object to our living in sin."

She laughed. "We won't be doing much in the way of sinning for awhile, Frank. Oh, I'm so glad you're here. I've wanted to call you a dozen times …"

"Just call me Frankie Nightingale. Now ring for the nurse, my darling, and let's go home."

"Just wait till I get my hands on that daughter of mine," said Lorna. "I'll give her the biggest hug in the world."

More Time To Talk

It seemed to Julia her mother's voice grew proportionately stronger as her eighty-five-year-old body grew weaker. Sitting in the doctor's waiting room was the ultimate trial. Her mother didn't make conversation. A tall, imposing figure, she put on a one-woman show for any available audience. Today that consisted of an obese elderly couple holding hands, a nervous looking young mother with a sleeping baby, a teenager with a face full of metal studs, and a tattooed muscular man wearing a black tee shirt above torn jeans.

"Now you take the children of today," she declared as she hung her cane on the back of her chair, "they're being neglected in the important things. They don't get piano lessons anymore. They sit around watching television or playing those endless video games. Or they're sending each other messages on those tiny little phones. In my day kids didn't have time for that. They had chores to do …"

Julia mumbled appropriate responses as her mother raced from topic to topic, pontificating before a disinterested roomful of patients. She prayed the receptionist would soon call out, "Mrs. Parkhurst." Then and only then would she be able to pick up a magazine, blend into the woodwork, and relax. At sixty-two, she was feeling more than a little put upon. Why couldn't she have had a brother or sister to help her cope? Why were her own two daughters living so far away? All of her sick days at the school were taken up by her mother's appointments. She needed a break, damn it all. She was no spring chicken herself. She smiled at the unspoken expression — one straight from her mother's lips. Her own husband, Julia reflected, hadn't been much help even when he was alive. He and her mother had never gotten along. Julia had been forever playing the role of peace maker. A role she'd often resented.

The soliloquy continued unabated. Back to children again. Babies, this time. "Their mothers dress them too warm. Look at that child. She shouldn't be wearing that heavy sweater in here. It's far too warm. I never dressed you too warm. No wonder the little ones get sick!"

She could be heard clearly all over the waiting room. Face burning, Julie rose and reached for a magazine on the low table in front of them. "Want one?" she asked.

"No, but don't let that stop you. You go ahead and read if you want to."

Julia tried to busy herself in the news magazine, but the familiar knot of guilt was forming in her stomach. Her mother's eyesight was failing. She couldn't read without a magnifying glass. Julia knew that. She closed the magazine.

"Your Aunt Betty's Tara was spoiled rotten. All those figure skating lessons. Ridiculous! Waste of money if you ask me. Figure skating is for the wealthy. Now if she'd put that money into piano lessons, I could see it."

It was the repetition that bothered Julia the most. Like Einstein's chauffeur was reputed to have been able to do, she could have delivered her mother's speeches for her, almost word for word. Every time they drove by St. Luke's Church, for instance, she could count on her mother remarking, "I used to walk all the way here from my apartment and think nothing of it."

But her mother hadn't yet exhausted the subject of figure skating. "People are too inclined to go along with the crowd," she was saying. "Just because Tara's friend took lessons …"

"Mom, that was thirty years ago."

"Maybe so, but people are still spending money they can't afford on those lessons. I once read somewhere that Elizabeth Manley's mother ended up twenty-six thousand dollars in debt."

Before Julia could reply, she was off on another of her favourite topics. This time it was the disgraceful way some guests carried on during talk shows. Then came the welcome summons.

"Mrs. Parkhurst!"

Julia sighed. Reprieved at last. Her mother thrust her black leather purse into Julia's waiting arms and, rising unsteadily, followed the receptionist inside. Earlier, she'd made it clear she wanted to see her doctor alone.

Julia pulled the silence around her and returned to her magazine.

But she couldn't concentrate. When they finished giving her mother the flu shot, there'd be the weekly shopping trip to the supermarket to be endured. Searching for the freshest looking produce. The inevitable hunt for coupons, the hold-up at the check out counter while her mother counted out pennies. Two widow women on a grocery buying spree. What fun! There had to more to life. Next week, the dental appointment. After that, the chiropodist. And no end in sight.

If only her mother weren't so uncomfortable with silence. Julia was by nature a quiet person. Why couldn't they just sit side by side in companionable silence once in awhile?

But that was mean-spirited, Julia reflected. Who else did her mother have to talk to? Her world was growing smaller day by day. Old friends were passing away. Life wasn't easy for her. She'd always been a gregarious person. Cheerfully outgoing. Her good qualities by far outnumbered her bad. For one thing, she was more compassionate than Julia knew herself to be. Always, she championed the underdog. The other residents in her apartment building had looked the other way when that drunk had passed out in their foyer. She had immediately summoned help for the old fellow.

Julia forced herself to return to the article she'd been trying to read, but as the minutes ticked by she began to feel uneasy. How could a simple flu shot possibly take this long? Was there something her mother wasn't telling her?

Julia looked at her watch. Almost half an hour had passed. She dropped the magazine on the empty chair beside her and hugged her mother's purse along with her own. What could be the holdup?

When she saw the doctor's young receptionist hurrying towards her, Julia's heart started going like a jackhammer.

"Your mother's feeling a bit faint," said the pink-uniformed girl.

"Should I come in?"

"No. She just wants her cane. She forgot it when she went in, and she says the broadloom in there is too thick for her. She can't keep her balance on it."

Julia rose on trembling legs as her mother emerged from the doctor's inner office. She was suddenly overwhelmed with love for the courageous white-haired old lady moving unsteadily towards her. She hadn't noticed until now that her mother was wearing the bright red earrings that matched her felt hat. She'd even put on a dash of lipstick and her best silk scarf for this outing. She always dressed carefully for her trips to town, as she called them. For visits to the doctor, she would don one of her best dresses, this time a navy one that Julia had given her for her last birthday.

Outside, spring sunlight was doing its best to brighten the day. Julia welcomed the pressure of her mother's arm on her own. It was comforting beyond words.

"Let's go to the mall for a cup of tea before I take you home," she said. "It will give us more time to talk."

The Love Letter

Slim Saunders couldn't pass a mirror without pausing briefly to admire his image. It seemed golden to him; he could easily understand his success with the fair sex. Father Time was certainly on his side. Though almost forty, he could pass for ten or fifteen years younger. Good teeth, great skin that tanned golden brown, firm body. No wonder he opted to remain single, he mused, free to prove the maxim about variety being the spice of life.

His first name was Sydney, but he'd been called Slim for years. It suited him, he thought. Never had to worry about any extra pounds on his six foot frame. And the girls all told him his navy blue eyes were to die for.

He'd invariably lose interest after each conquest, ending the relationship with the words, "It isn't you, it's me." His buddies at the college had nicknamed him 'Hit and Run Saunders'. He bragged that he could bed any unattached female within hours of meeting her.

"Not the pretty young English professor," argued his friend Jake. "I've been up to bat three times and struck out. She's the original Ice Queen."

Slim chuckled. "Frosty Fiona. Well, many are cold, but few are frozen. She doesn't turn me on, but I could win her if I wanted to."

"Fifty bucks says you couldn't."

"You're on. How much time do I have?"

"A week should suffice for a lothario like you, Slim."

"Piece of cake. As Trudeau famously said, 'Just watch me'."

As it turned out, Slim was glad Jake *wasn't* watching. His first two advances were firmly rebuffed by Fiona. He began to fear he too might strike out. He approached her warily on the third day. "Won't you at least let me take you out to dinner?" he asked. "After all, a girl has to eat."

She eyed him up and down. Her large brown eyes seemed to appraise him and find him wanting. "Your reputation does you no credit," she said. "But I might be persuaded — by a love letter."

Slim stared at her. "A love letter? Are you joking?"

"A real, old-fashioned love letter," she repeated. "Like the ones Robert Browning wrote to Elizabeth Barrett."

"I'll e-mail one you one."

"That won't do. I want you to write it by hand and push it under the door of my office this afternoon. I want it to be romantic. Signed, sealed, and delivered."

What the hell, Slim thought. First time for everything. He went into his office after his last class and picked up his pen. 'My Dearest Fiona,' he wrote, 'whenever I see you, I feel like I've come to the end of a long drought. You sweet smile beckons, your moist lips were made for kissing. I thirst for them the way a man lost in the desert craves water. Without you, my life is arid. I could drown in the melted chocolate of your beautiful brown eyes.' He went on in that vein for a few sentences and signed it with a flourish.

Easy as cutting butter with a hot knife, Slim decided, as he pushed the envelope under Fiona's door at three-thirty. She'll be putty in my hands after she reads this masterpiece.

The next morning as he approached the fifty mailboxes belonging to the college's staff, he noticed a flurry of activity. Every box had a pale blue sheet sticking out of it. Must be some sort of special notice, he decided. Several instructors began reading them, glancing his way, and chuckling. He reached for the sheet in his own niche. One look at it and he froze. It was a Xeroxed copy of his love letter. On the upper right hand corner Fiona had scrawled D minus in large letters.

Two Grand Mothers

Frowning, Frances Parker applies a fresh coat of pink lipstick. Her make-up has to be perfect. She wants to look her very best for Bob.

Finished, she smiles hopefully at her image. When had that little line appeared across the bridge of her nose? She's never noticed it before. But at least her chestnut-brown hair holds no trace of grey. Perhaps an extra stroke of blush to bring out the blue of her eyes. She sighs, thinking of the afternoon ahead at Amy Cook's farm. Amy and Fred Cook, her dear old friends. She hopes Bob will like them. Perhaps the romantic atmosphere of the June night on the drive home will give him ideas. He might just get around to proposing. And if he does, her answer will be an unqualified yes.

After one last smile at herself, Frances starts along the hallway. The voice of her grandson calls out, "Where's Grandma?"

At once, Frances feels a decade older than her forty-six years. No use waiting. She will talk to her daughter while she drives her and Jeffie home. She's certain Holly will understand.

Frances pauses by the full-length mirror fronting her linen closet. She does look slimmer. The new diet had taken tons of will power, but it was worth it. In her embroidered white sun dress, she could pass for thirty-nine, Bob's age.

"Here I am, honey," she cries, scooping up her grandson. "Time to get into the car."

Frances finds the subject difficult to broach, but once she's begun, her own arguments convince her there is nothing unreasonable in what she's asking. "I can't get used to being called Grandma, Holly. It makes me feel ancient."

"But, Mum, what do you want him to call you? He can't very well call you Frances."

"Why not?"

"You're not serious."

"He could use my old nickname."

"Frankie? That would sound silly."

"Well at least it wouldn't make me feel like I should be wearing an apron, baking cookies, or sitting in a rocking chair knitting socks."

"Lots of your friends are grandmothers. "Didn't you tell me Amy Cook's daughter is due any day now? You said she sounded pretty happy about it."

"That's different. Amy *looks* like a grandmother. Besides, she's not trying to get a husband. She already has one. Holly, you can't imagine how lonely I've been since your dad passed away. All those happy years we shared. I have to try to find that kind of life again. But Bob isn't likely to propose to someone who's being called 'Grandmaw' all the time."

"Doesn't he know how old you are?"

"Of course. We've talked about the age difference. He says it doesn't matter to him, that six years is nothing. But I don't want him to be reminded that he's going out with a grandmother. Try to understand, Holly."

"All right, if that's the way you want it." They drive in silence until they reach Holly's house. "It seems a shame," her daughter declares as she lifts the boy out of his car seat. "He's only just learned to pronounce his 'r's properly"

"He has to use an 'r' in 'Frankie' too," Frances reminds her. "Thanks for coming to church with me, dear. And tell that son-in-law of mine I hope his cold is better by next Sunday." She winks, but her daughter fails to acknowledge their little joke.

"Kiss Grandma!" Jeff demands.

Frances reaches down to hug him, thinking how sweet he looks, his brown hair curling damply against his forehead, his big brown eyes shining. He still has that wonderful baby smell. "Jeffie," she murmurs, "call me Frankie. Can you say Frankie?"

The child studies her with his dark, solemn eyes. "Fwankie," he repeats slowly.

Frances begins to laugh, but the expression on Holly's face stops her. "I'd better go," she says. "Bob's car's in the garage, so I told him I'd pick him up. I'm running late."

As she drives off, Frances glances up at her rear-view mirror. Holly and Jeff are standing on the sidewalk, hand in hand, as though frozen in time.

She'll be fine when she gets used to the idea, Frances tells herself. But she's filled with misgiving as she draws up in front of Bob's apartment building. She honks once, and he comes striding out, a big, sandy-haired man, casual in a maroon sweater and grey slacks.

"You're never on time," he accuses. "But that's okay. It gave me time to finish up those plans for the new filtering system at the plant. You know — that project I was telling you about the other night."

"How do you like my new dress? Frances asks.

"You look perfect," he replies. "You always look perfect."

Somehow the words don't sound like a compliment.

"Bob, we can turn right at the next street if we want a short cut. Or we can drive out along the river. It's longer, but the scenery's worth it."

"Take the short cut. We're already late."

His words are brusque. Frances begins to feel the whole world is against her.

They've been driving for some time before he speaks again. "What's she like, this old friend of yours?"

"Amy? I guess the word 'motherly' would best describe her. She was a city girl, but twenty years ago she married a farmer. She's had to work pretty hard ever since." Frances can't help thinking of the way Amy has let herself go. She'd been so pretty. Now she doesn't even bother colouring her grey hair. Or wearing make-up.

Finally they're turning into the long laneway leading to the Cooks' red brick farmhouse. Amy meets them at the front door, wiping her hands on a blue and white tea towel. "Guess what?" she cries. "My son-in-law just called. I'm a grandma! A baby girl! Sorry, Frances. I could at least have waited for introductions. I'm just so excited. Well, You already know what a great feeling it is, Fran."

They follow her through the house into the big kitchen, where she removes a kettle of bubbling jam from the stove. The air is filled with the tangy odour of wild strawberries. "Fred won't be back till three," she says, "and I just had to tell somebody." She stirs the rich, red jam with a wooden ladle. "Imagine, Fred and I. Grandma and Grandpa!"

Amy removes her apron, tosses it over the back of a chair, and puts on the kettle for tea.

"I am happy for you," says Frances. "But tell the truth, doesn't this make you feel older? Being a grandmother I mean."

Amy seems amused by the question. "Why should it? I'm only one day older today than I was yesterday."

"But you have a grandchild. Doesn't that make you feel different?"

Amy ladles jam into a small dish to cool. "It does. It makes me feel wonderful!"

"Wait till that baby starts calling you 'Grandmaw'. You'll know what I mean then."

Amy's hazel eyes light up. "I'll be proud as our Bantam rooster," she replies with an infectious laugh.

"I'll bet you're the youngest looking grandma for miles around," Bob remarks.

Frances stares at him. There is no mistaking his expression. It's one of sincere admiration. She changes the subject. "Amy, where in the world did you get enough wild strawberries to make all this jam?"

"Picked them in the woods out back. They're fiddly little things and they take a long time, but the result's worth it."

"The good things in life are always worth the trouble," Bob agrees.

A picture of Holly and Jeff flashes through Frances's mind. They'd looked so forlorn standing there, watching her drive away. She hoped she hadn't driven them away with her silly request to use her old nickname. "May I use your phone, Amy? I have to call my daughter."

"Go ahead," her friend says, setting a plate of warm biscuits on the table.

Alone in the big front hall of the farmhouse, Frances reaches up to call, then pauses, wondering if she is being hasty. No, she decides. Her daughter answers on the second ring. "Holly?"

"Yes, Frances — or should I call you Frankie?" comes the reply, the words coated with ice.

All indecision vanishes. "Honey, I'm sorry. I was wrong. I don't know what I was thinking. Forgive me?"

"Of course, Mum. I felt hurt at first, but then I decided you were just going through one of your phases."

Frances is amused at the old saying she'd often used when Holly was a teenager. It had become a joke with them — a line that often ended their occasional disagreements.

When she returns to the kitchen, Bob looks up. "Taste this jam!" he exclaims, slathering some onto a warm biscuit for her.

"And spoil my diet ..." she begins. But before his expression has time to change, she takes it from him. "Hang my diet! How often does a person get a chance to enjoy real homemade wild strawberry jam?"

"Good for you, Frankie!" he cheers. "You don't mind if I call you that, do you? I heard Amy use it when you were on the phone, and I like it. It suits you."

"So do I, Bob. It makes me feel young again."

"You are young. You and Amy both make great grandmothers."

"Hey, not *great* yet," Amy protests, chuckling.

"I meant great looking grandmothers," he says, reaching for another biscuit.

Frances smiles. Maybe she'll be able to talk him into taking the scenic route home. The long way. One that will give her a chance to ask him about the new filtering system he was designing for the plant where he worked. A second chance.

Ties That Bind

Nora Malone sits immobile in her perfect living room. Like a stone.

"Honey, he'll call. I know he'll call." Her husband's face is furrowed with lines of worry, lines that seem to Nora to have appeared since this morning.

"Why should he? This isn't a home anymore. It's a museum. I've made it one."

"It doesn't have to be. Kelly wouldn't have wanted it this way."

Nora covers her eyes and lowers her head. Awkwardly, Ned puts an arm around her thin shoulders. He's a big man, twice her size, and he has always treated her like a porcelain doll. He draws a ragged breath. Old words drift through his consciousness. "Comfort thyself, what comfort is in me?"

Kelly looked so much like her mother. Dark clouds of curls around a heart-shaped face. Blue-eyed and delicate. But filled with the joy of living, of being young. A year now, and still so difficult … so impossible.

Nora unfolds the crumpled note. "I didn't mean to drive him away. He's all we have now. My God, Ned, he's all we have."

"I know, I know. It isn't your fault, Nora. It isn't anybody's fault. I didn't understand it at first. I do now. Cleaning the house from top to bottom every day … well, I guess that was your way of coping."

"I felt if I got tired enough maybe I'd be able to sleep."

"It made life hard for Kevin and me. We're naturally sloppy guys, I suppose."

"Airplanes crash all the time," she murmurs. "You don't pay much attention, really. You never think it will happen to your own. To think she was coming home for Christmas. And now, another Christmas coming …"

"Nora, we have to find Kevin. We'll have to be strong for him. Get me the phone book. And a pen. I'm going to start calling all his friends. One of them must know something."

"All he said in the note was good-bye, that he'd call us sometime. Ned, it could be months …"

She rises like an automaton and heads for her spotless kitchen. Even the junk drawer is neat. She stares down at it for long moments. Then she reaches in and takes a pen from a pile of them held together by a rubber band. She throws the elastic band on the floor and jumbles up the contents of the drawer. Only then is she able to cry.

* * *

At the same time, Kevin Malone is making his way along the crowded sidewalk, head lowered to shield his face from the cruel December wind. At the corner of Yonge and Queen he glances up as an ancient derelict accosts him, gnarled hand extended, palm up. Kevin drops a quarter in it, averting his eyes as the old man hawks noisily and spits. "How about a loonie, Sonny? You can spare a loonie, can't you?"

Kevin feels his stomach lurch as he regards the man's matted mass of long grey beard threaded with phlegm. How does a person reach this state? he wonders. An inner voice tells him, "Stay a runaway and find out."

He hurries on. Maybe running away was a dumb idea. He doesn't have much money. He sure doesn't want to join the street kids. They look totally bummed out. But he doesn't want to go home either. His parents are totally impossible. His dad with that long face all the time. And his mother! House proud, she calls it. Says she can't help it. Wants everything just so. A place for everything and everything in its place. Well, she can have her clean house. It'll be neat as a pin without him there to mess it up.

A blare of Christmas music escapes through the open doorway of a record store. Kevin is swept into a vortex of Yuletide memories. He and Kelly singing their own version of Jingle Bells … tearing corners of gift wrap to sneak peeks at presents, having sword fights with giant candy canes, their parents laughing, caught up in the spirit of the season, having fun. Christmas chaos everywhere, food and drink in the living room, lots of toys making lots of noise, red and green ribbons hanging from the chandelier above the dining room table groaning under its weight of Christmas goodies. Of course, that was when Kelly was part of the festivities. His beautiful big sister, a straight A student in her first year of university.

Everything changed after Kelly was gone. His father withdrawn, his mother a human vacuum cleaner.

Kevin shivers. He has to get out of this cold for awhile. He decides to spend some of his precious cash on a cheeseburger and a coffee.

Inside the restaurant, he takes his backpack off his aching shoulders and sets it on the seat beside him. He wonders if his mother's found the note. Most likely. She'd notice anything out of place in five seconds flat. He hopes she's good and sorry. After all, she's not the only one who misses Kelly. Sometimes he wonders if she wishes it had been him instead of his sister. Sometimes he wishes it *had* been him.

He looks around. The place is crowded with people of all ages, but he's overwhelmed with a sense of being all alone. The silver and gold Christmas bells festooning the ceiling make him feel even worse. He has to swallow hard to get down the first bite of his burger.

The way she'd yelled at him! Just because he'd left a stupid wad of Kleenex in his jeans when she'd done the laundry yesterday. Little bits of white tissue all over her last load of washing. Big deal. She'd acted like it was a capital offence or something. Screaming like she was out of control. He'd show her. He didn't have to take that crap. He'd manage on his own. Get a job. Be independent. Stay out late every night. Track in mud. Throw his clothes on the floor if he felt like it.

Kevin's eyes are betraying him. They keep coming to rest on the public telephone not far from where he's sitting. He can't stop thinking about those wonderful long-ago Christmas holidays. Maybe he should at least call — let them know he's okay. But he won't give in, won't go crawling back …

A boy around his own age is beginning to clear the table. He's holding a damp cloth in one hand.

"Yeah, take it away. I'm not as hungry as I thought."

Anxious for conversation, Kevin tries to think of something else to say. "Looks like we'll have a white Christmas."

The redheaded bus boy glances at the window. "It's beginning to snow now." He grins. "I'm off work after tonight. Going home for the holidays. You too?" he asks, eyeing the backpack.

Kevin returns his smile. "Don't know. Gotta make a phone call." He picks up his pack. "Have a good time, eh!"

"Thanks. You, too. Take care."

The operator's voice has a precise, impersonal sound. "Will you accept a collect call from Kevin Malone? Press one for yes, press …"

His mother's "yes" is filled with excitement, with warmth and welcome. She starts to talk even before the operator tells them to go ahead. "Kevin! Are you all right? Where are you?"

"I'm in Toronto, Mom. I'm fine."

"Come home, Kevie. We need you."

She has not called him Kevie for years. It moves him, makes him feel like a child again.

"Here's your dad. Please, please come home."

His father's first question is practical. "Do you have enough money for the train?"

"Yeah, I do. But I don't know, Dad. I don't know if I can take any more …"

"You won't have to, son. Things will be different. I promise you. Come home. We're a family. We'll get through this together."

Kevin glances at his watch — an expensive one his parents gave him for his sixteenth birthday last month. "I can still make the ten-thirty train, Dad. Union Station isn't far from here. I won't get there till after midnight, though. You and Mom shouldn't wait up."

"You must be kidding. We'll be at the station to meet you. With bells on. Christmas bells. Just be there."

Kevin relaxes. Christmas of ninety-eight was going to be all right. Not like other Christmases, for sure. But all right.

It's snowing harder as he heads down Yonge Street. He has a subway token left, but he wants to walk, wants to feel the big, white flakes landing all over him, melting on his face. He grins as he gazes up at the darkening sky between the tall buildings lining the street. It looks like the angels are doing a huge batch of laundry and have forgotten to take the tissues out of the pockets.

Paddy And Pops

It took Sis and me almost three months to convince Pops that he should go back to the old country to visit his brother Bill, the last surviving member of his family and the uncle after whom I'm named.

Pops kept protesting that we'd never be able to get along without him — that some catastrophe or other was bound to occur the very minute he set foot on the ship. He refused to even discuss the possibility of flying. If he was not setting foot on anything, it was a plane he was not setting foot on.

Sis kept bringing home dozens of attractive brochures from the travel agency where she worked, showing how she could set him up a package deal for Ireland that would be a real bargain. "After all, Pops," she'd argue, "you're not getting any younger. You should spend some time with your only remaining brother."

"We got lots o' years t'remain yet," Pops would insist, his boney chin stuck out at a stubborn angle. "Aint that right, Paddy?" he'd demand, looking to his dog for confirmation. The big Irish Setter would come over to nuzzle a cold nose against his waiting hand.

Sis and I would smile at each other and shrug. Paddy never responded like that for us. He'd been a one-man dog from the start. We'd bought him six years earlier — just a few weeks after Mother, God rest her soul, passed away from the weak heart that had kept her an invalid for years. Paddy and Pops have been fast friends ever since. They still go out on regular hunting trips, though they rarely flush a bird. Still, at their advanced ages, they're lucky to bag even the odd partridge.

Pops married late in life, the way so many Irishmen do. A matter of economic necessity, you might say. He and Mother emigrated to Canada just before I was born. In three years, they'd saved enough money for the down payment on this house. Most of my friends can't wait to get away from home, but I'm twenty-four now, Sis two years younger, and neither of us has felt any great urge to leave. It's comfortable in this ramshackle old three-storey house. Even though the grounds are big, Pops is still able to keep the grass cut and the roses blooming — both of which he's sure we'd never be able to accomplish in his absence.

Finally, on the last day of August, our united efforts paid off. After a tearful good-bye to us, and most of all to his loyal friend Paddy, Pops did set foot on a ship bound for Ireland and a six-week visit with his brother Bill. His last words were that we should take good care of his dog, his roses, his lawn, and ourselves. But as he leaned over the ship's rail shaking his halo of white hair, he looked decidedly gloomy about our chances of success.

Pops' prediction that disaster would strike the minute he left proved to be inaccurate. It didn't strike until three hours later — when we set Paddy's daily meal on the floor in front of him.

The big dog looked it over and stumbled apathetically back to the corner of the kitchen beside Pops' rocking chair. No amount of persuasion would induce him to rise again.

"He'll get over it in a day or two," Sis declared, a ring of false cheerfulness in her voice.

I didn't know what to say — or do. Paddy meant the world and all to Pops, and we both knew it.

Ten days later we had a long letter from Pops, extolling the virtues of Dublin in general, and Uncle Bill's place in particular. His sister-in-law, Kathleen, whom he'd never before met, was "as fine a woman as ever graced God's green earth". He went on to say he should have made the trip long ago — that his six weeks would be gone all too soon.

We called, telling him everything was fine; we had no heart to tell him Paddy was but a canine ghost of his former self.

As the days went by and the big setter showed no signs of snapping out of his lethargy, we began to get desperate. One night after work, instead of stopping in with the guys for my usual pint, I hurried to the Valley Supermarket and bought the largest, juiciest steak I could find. Sis cooked it and we presented it to Paddy with great hopes. But the rusty red setter remained adamantly blue.

I was out of patience. "Damn stubborn dog!" I shouted. "What are we going to do with you?"

"Swearing won't help," Sis declared.

"What will help? You tell me, then we'll both know."

She reached down to stroke Paddy's thin neck, then slowly straightened up. "Maybe we should call Pops to come home."

"Wouldn't do any good now. At this rate, Paddy wouldn't last till he got here. Look at him — he's so weak he can barely lift his head."

"If only we could coax him into getting up — out of that corner and into fresh air. That's what he needs."

"We've tried everything. What more can we do?"

The next morning, we received another letter from Pops. He was still having himself one whale of a time, he wrote, but he was beginning to miss us — especially Paddy, he added with his customary touch of wry humor. But we knew there was more than a grain of truth in the statement.

We tried again to coax Paddy to his feet. No luck. The big dog just stared at us from the corner that had become his last will and testament.

A couple of days later, around noon on Saturday, Sis came to me with tears in her eyes. "Billy," she said, "you've got to do something about Paddy. He's a living skeleton. I can't bear to see him like this. He's suffering. You'll have to put him out of his misery."

Glancing down at the poor animal, I was forced to agree. But my heart was heavy and my mind in turmoil as I went upstairs to fetch Pops' shotgun.

We were waiting at the dock when Pops returned. As soon as we'd exchanged hugs of welcome, he rubbed his hands together. "Now to get home t' me Paddy," he said.

"I had the strangest experience over there," Pops went on as we piled into my car. "On a Saturday it was. I was strollin' in Bill and Kathleen's garden, about five in the afternoon, the sun warm on me face, when all of a sudden it was like a dark cloud passin' over me. I was that frightened! But after a few seconds, a cool breeze touched me cheek."

Sis and I exchanged meaningful glances.

As we turned into our wide, tree-lined street, Pops added, half under his breath, "I think that breeze must o' bin a leprechaun, come t' tell me everythin' was all right."

"You always maintained you didn't believe in leprechauns," I accused.

"Sure, I don't. Never have." After a few seconds he added quietly, "They're over there, all the same."

When we reached the house, I parked the car and we started up the front walk. Paddy came bounding out to meet us, all waggy-tailed and wet-nosed, so overjoyed to see Pops he nearly sent the three of us flying.

Pops leaned down to pat him. "You've gotten a mite thin, old fellow."

"He's been pining for you," I explained.

Sis gave me a big grin and I thought again of the Saturday morning when, in desperation, I'd fetched the shotgun. As soon as Paddy had seen it, he'd struggled to his feet, thinking he was going hunting. I'd taken him for a jaunt in the woods behind our house. By the time we'd returned, his appetite had too.

But who knows? Maybe a leprechaun really did have something to do with it. As Pops says, even if you don't believe in them, they're over there all the same.

The Cornfield

The times they were a changing but they never changed for me. The two lives separated, then fused, then separated again. My brother kept telling me I was paranoid and I was convinced he was right. You're right, David Lloyd. You're right, right, right. Still living at home in my thirty-third year from heaven. Not at home, though. Never at home in this alien land. Just visiting, thank you. Just browsing. Wrap it up — I'll take it with me. Don't bother wrapping it; I'll eat it here.

She looks after me; he leaves me alone. It works out very well. They're old now, but they're younger than I. Younger than I ever was — even before all the trips.

A middle-aged man watches from the mirror when I shave. His eyes are cold. When he makes me nervous, I cut myself. I cut myself a lot. Once I cut both my wrists. They said the blood was terrible. I didn't want to die, though. I just wanted to kill myself. It's not the same thing.

If I'm really paranoid, how can I hold down my job at the college? With both feet. That's funny. My students don't even realize I'm crazy. I'm *controlled*, that's why. It's all a matter of control.

Each morning when I drive around that turn that faces the cornfield I think I'll keep going straight on — straight into the cornfield. It looks so tall and green, so secretly inviting. I used to tell my secrets to the corn. But that was in another life. When I lived on a farm. I think it must have been a long time ago.

There was a wife once. And there was a baby. They were both girls. I don't know what happened to them. Don't ask me anything about it. I don't want to think about what happened to them. Their hair was the color of corn-silk.

I'm late this morning and the man in the mirror is angry. His grey eyes are colder than usual; they look like my brother's eyes. Last year I dropped the middle initial from my name. I keep dispensing with these trivial details. Nobody ever notices the loss. Nobody has ever asked me what happened to my middle initial. They didn't ask me about the wisdom tooth either. Or the piece of fool's gold I used to keep in a matchbox. I had the seat belts taken out of my car last winter. A silent protest. It seemed the least I could do.

I've cut myself again. A splash of red against the yellow sink. A piece of yellow toilet paper against the red blood. The paper can't hold it back. The stain wavers and grows, covering the entire face, filling the sink, the bathtub, covering the floor, thudding in silent waves against the door. The grey eyes are the last to go under.

"Peter."

Someone has called my name. It's time to begin another play. Another day, another play. A diller a dollar a paranoid scholar.

"Coming."

The voice sounds amazingly normal. The blood disappears. I put down the razor. I am ready.

Things keep increasing in unimportance. At first it was only the unimportant things that lost all significance. Now it has reached the point where nothing is important. Nothing at all. All of the so-called important things have become unimportant. I can't even remember what they were, what they once might have meant.

I've been counting footsteps again. I count them often, but they never add up to anything. I keep forgetting where I'm at. It's thirty-nine steps to the kitchen.

The old woman is whistling as she hobbles from the stove to the table. It looks … what is the word I want? Incongruous. Yes. To my knowledge, she has never whistled before. The old man sits in his chair by the window, saying nothing.

Something brown is on the plate in front of me. The hand lifts the fork, the mouth chews. The stomach digests. The feet move to the door, to the car. The hand turns the key in the ignition. We are making splendid progress, Peter. Splendid progress indeed.

Man and car back out of the driveway, move slowly along the street. Red light. The foot touches the brake. Green light. The foot moves from the brake to the gas. And so it goes. Start. Stop. Start.

Cornfield. The foot moves from the brake to the gas. The foot presses hard on the gas. The car leaves the dangerous road and heads for the safety of the cornfield.

Night Of Wine And Roses

Muriella's drama students are getting short shrift, dutifully going through their assigned performances while her mind is elsewhere. Duncan's final words keep pushing themselves into her consciousness. *Self-centred bitch.* It isn't true, damn it. She's a caring person. Any one of her students can tell you that. Duncan didn't appreciate her. That was the problem. But how is she going to go on living without him? She has only to close her eyes and she can picture him holding her, nibbling her neck the way he used to …

"Miss Vandermeer!"

She realizes one of the girls has been trying to get her attention. Muriella sees at once the reason for concern. Bernie Franklin's quartet is performing, two of them pretending to stop him from beating up a big-bosomed girl with stringy black hair. Bernie is putting far too much into the exercise.

"That's it for tonight," she shouts, glancing at her watch. "I just have time to give you next week's assignment."

The youth fakes a last kick to the girl's groin that makes Muriella start forward. Under the fluorescent lighting of the gym, Bernie's brown eyes reflect a disturbing intensity.

"Okay, the Oscar's yours, Bernie. Now break it up. First act of *The Serpent* next week. Bernie, I said stop it. Right now."

The boy's eyes regain their customary brown solemnity as he drops his arms and turns to her, brushing a fringe of thick black hair from his forehead. She notices that he is growing a moustache; she thinks it makes him look somewhat like the leading man in a porno film. The thought causes her to smile. He returns the smile, mumbling, "Sorry, Teach. I got a little carried away for a minute there."

"You really throw yourself into a role. Who were you beating up?"

He regards her wordlessly as the other students struggle into winter jackets and loop colourful scarves around their necks. Muriella begins to gather up her books.

"My stepmother."

He speaks the words in so quiet a voice that for a moment she isn't sure she's heard them. "What's that?"

"I pretended I was killing my stepmother."

He fumbles in his shirt pocket for a cigarette. After his second unsuccessful attempt at lighting it, she reaches forward, takes the matches from his hand, and holds a steady flame before him. The others have left. They are quite alone. Bernie pulls deeply on the smoke. "Sorry, Teach. I didn't mean to upset you."

"I don't think I'm the one we should be worrying about." She picks up her beige leather coat and he hurries to help her on with it. The pressure of his hands remains a few seconds too long on her shoulders. She grabs her briefcase.

"Would you have a coffee with me, Teach?"

The words tumble out in a rush just as they are leaving the building. It probably wouldn't be wise, thinks Muriella. But he looks so forlorn, so lost. And she's feeling lonely herself. Duncan shouldn't have walked out on her like that. Just because she had the abortion without telling him first. It's her body, after all. And Dunc really liked kids. He'd have tried to talk her out of it. She'd never told him in so many words, but she didn't want ever to be tied down with a family. Anyway, a coffee break sounded good. "There's a Tim Horton's just around the corner," she said.

"I know. Bim Tits."

"What?"

He looks embarrassed. "We used to say that for Tim Bits. A sort of joke."

For a moment, she hesitates. An inner voice tells her to leave him alone, he's just a kid after all. But when she searches his face, she finds him more than a little attractive. His smile is so warm, so sweet. Just a little fun, she thinks, I won't let it go too far.

They sit close together at a corner table, a loaded silence between them. Muriella breaks it with a sudden question.

"How old are you, Bernie?"

"I turned nineteen last week."

"Do you have a girl?"

When he doesn't answer, she begins to murmur an apology about being too personal, but he stops her with a wave of his hand. "Girls don't go for me. I seem to frighten them off. Maybe it's because I can't, you know, make with the small talk like the other guys. Look at all the girls in this class and I can't get anywhere with any of them."

"I haven't noticed you try."

He toys with his spoon. "I never know how to start a conversation."

"You're doing all right now."

"Yeah, but this is different …"

"Meaning I'm not a girl?"

A touch of crimson creeps beneath the olive skin across his high cheekbones.

"I'm not exactly ancient, you know. Just because I'm the teacher …"

All at once he reaches down to touch her hand. "I like being with you, Miss Vanderveer. I feel comfortable. I feel like I can talk to you … I mean, really talk …"

"About what's troubling you? That business about your stepmother?"

He nods. "Only not here."

"Would you like to come up to my place where we can talk in private?" Her heart is racing as she asks the question.

Bernie studies the bottom of his coffee mug. "I don't know. It's kind of late."

"I only want to help you."

"I know that, Miss Vandermeer."

"Then come along."

She pays the bill before he has a chance to fish the change from his pocket.

* * *

"I always wanted to be taken for a ride in a real live Jaguar," he jokes as they speed through the night in her gleaming black sports car.

"This is the very first thing I bought when I started teaching," she says, giving him a smile made secret by their proximity. "The night classes pay for the gas."

Once inside her apartment, Bernie appears to be at a loss for words. Muriella relieves him of his brown suede jacket, steers him toward the gold velvet sofa in her small living room, and goes to get a bottle of chilled Madeira from her refrigerator. He's of age. One little drink won't hurt.

"To help you relax," she says, handing him a well filled goblet.

"I'll drink to that."

Muriella kicks off her high-heeled boots, perches on the arm of the sofa, and sips her drink as she studies him. He's dressed in the old-fashioned style some teenagers affect, but on him the clothing looks exactly right, as though he belongs to another time and place. Edwardian England, perhaps. He's incredibly slim. Probably eats like a stevedore, too. She envies his small waistline, his solid, flat abdomen. Despite Spartan eating habits, her own body is beginning to bulge in all the wrong places. How would it feel to have his hard young arms encircle her? Two weeks and five days now since Dunc has walked out of her life. Maybe she *had* been too demanding, too possessive. But he was the right man for her. She'd known that the very first time they made love. Somehow she would have to get him to come back to her. He hadn't returned her key. That was a good sign, wasn't it?

"You're miles away," Bernie accuses.

His lips are full, she notes. The sensual kind. The kind made for kissing. Stop this, she tells herself. He's just a kid. And a deeply troubled one at that. She's supposed to be trying to help him, get him to talk about his problems. "What did you mean?" she begins, "about pretending that girl was your stepmother?"

"Nice place you've got here," he hedges. "Who did all the art work? I really like that one across from us. Sort of a nude, but you don't see the woman's body at first, just a lot of red roses."

"I did most of that stuff in my freshman year. Let me get you another glass of wine, Bernie." She leans toward him, noticing a faint scent of perspiration mixed with something else, something almost feral. For a moment she feels dizzy.

When she returns, she sits beside him on the sofa, drinking in the strangely intoxicating odour along with her Madeira. He's still discussing the painting on the wall opposite them. She is finding it difficult to keep her mind focussed on his words.

"Just the roses at first," he's observing. Then you see the woman's body. After that you can't see anything else. Is it oil or acrylic?"

" It's oil. Bernie, will your people be worried about your being out this late?"

"No. Tomorrow's Saturday."

"Maybe you should call them …"

"A fine, full-bodied potion. I like full bodies. Miss Vandermeer, I like it here." He drains his goblet and holds it out to her, smiling. "Maybe just another splash," the thin black moustache moves back into place as he becomes serious once more. "I mean that. I do like it here. I feel comfortable with you."

"Comfortable enough to tell me why you wanted to kill your stepmother?"

When he makes no reply she takes the glass and goes out to her kitchenette. She's beginning to feel a little light headed. It really wouldn't be safe for her to drive him home. Why not let him spend the night? They could relax, and he might be able to tell her what was bothering him. Nineteen years old. Just half her age. God, how can she be so close to forty? Two sisters and a brother all older. When had they stopped calling her the baby of the family?

She's carrying the bottle along with their glasses when she returns. "Are you an only child?" she asks.

"I have twin sisters. Fifteen years old. She never bothered them."

"She?"

"My wicked stepmother. Whenever the two of us were home alone she used to parade around the house stripped naked to the waist. It started when I was thirteen. I couldn't take my eyes off those bouncing boobs."

"Did she ever, you know, touch you?"

"Touch me? Hell, she never stopped. Until six months ago, that is. That's when she got off the sauce. Hoo-ray for the good old AA." He pours a drink, downs it in a flash, and refills both their glasses.

"Call home, Bernie. Tell them you're staying over with a friend. I'll get you a blanket and you can sleep right here on the sofa."

He rises unsteadily. "Where's the phone?"

"In the kitchen. There's another bottle of wine in the fridge. Bring it with you when you come back."

"Yes, ma'm."

"Don't call me ma'm."

"Yes, Miss Vandermeer. He pauses at the doorway. "What is your first name, anyway?"

"Muriella. I think my father got it from an old cigar box."

"Muuuriellla," he drawls. Chuckling, he repeats it, rolling the name around on his tongue.

"Make sure you sound perfectly sober," she cautions.

"No sweat. My old man's outta town and she's too dumb to know the difference."

Muriella puts on one of her compact discs and the sweet nostalgia of a violin fills the room with the melody of *The Days of Wine and Roses*. She considers looking for music he'd appreciate but by the time she gets up he's exclaiming, "Jesus, that's some background for when I say I'm spending the night with a friend."

She leans back, laughing. "I wasn't thinking."

"Doesn't matter. Like I said, she's not all that bright. She claims taking on a widower with three kids was too much for her. Drove her to drink. Beautiful but dumb." He sets the bottle on the coffee table. "Matter of fact, she's not all that beautiful. Big teeth and long black hair. But she's built. I'll say that for her. Christ, is she built."

"Didn't your father ever see what was going on?"

"If he did, he never let on. His job takes him out of town a lot. I guess people see what they want to see."

"It must have been a relief for you when she quit drinking."

"Relief? Jesus, no, anything but. I used to scheme to get her alone. But when the drinking stopped, everything stopped." He drains his glass. "Now she tries to mother me. She's even started feeding me vitamins, for Christ's sake. I hate having her treat me like a kid. I'm not a kid anymore. I'm a man, goddammit." He reaches for a cigarette. "I don't know why I'm telling you all this."

"I only want to help you." She holds a table lighter out to him. His dark eyes shine in its reflected light. "What was your birth mother like?" she asks. "Do you remember her?"

"I was only seven when she was killed in the accident. My old man was driving, but everybody said it wasn't his fault. They were going to a dance. I remember she smelled like those flowers that have a lot of little white bells on one stem."

"Lily-of-the-valley."

"That's it. She was from Quebec. She used to sing a lot, little French songs. Sometimes I think I remember bits of them."

Muriella feels an almost magnetic pull towards him. His dark hair is mussed, and he has unbuttoned the top of his brown silk shirt. "Do you mind if I ask you a really personal question, Bernie?"

"Fire away."

"Has your stepmother actually had intercourse with you?"

"Of course. Started when I was fourteen."

"How did you feel the first time it happened?"

"Great. Like I'd just climbed Mount Everest."

"No regrets?"

"None. I couldn't get enough of it. I used to hope the old man would be called out of town so I could be with her."

"In spite of the age difference?"

"In spite of everything. Why are you asking so many questions?"

"I want to help you," she replies, moving closer. She breathes in the scent of him, lost in the chocolate brown of his eyes, eyes the same colour as Duncan's. She leans her head against his shoulder, takes his small hand in hers.

When he speaks again there's a tremor in his voice. "You have pretty hair. It's the palest blonde I've ever seen. It's natural, too, right?"

"Courtesy of my Dutch ancestry," she murmurs.

He twines a lock around his finger, pulls her to him, and kisses her lips, his tongue exploring her mouth, pushing, probing …

"You mustn't," she protests weakly, a small danger signal clicking in her mind. "You mustn't, Bernie."

"Why not?"

"Because I like it so much."

He moans as he holds her against him. She trembles in his arms, hungry for his body, needing him beyond thinking now. They take off their clothes as though moving in a dream, pausing to kiss often.

"The light," she begins.

"I want it on. Leave it on."

The music is still playing. They sink back into the gold sofa. His body feels very small against her own, but he soon makes her forget that, forget everything, almost makes her forget to give him the condom she'd tucked into her pocket earlier.

With her physical release, a large measure of sobriety returns. She stands up and struggles back into her red woolen dress. The music has stopped. Bernie gazes up at her. "I love you," he says.

She almost tells him not to be silly but checks herself in time. No need to hurt his feelings. Oddly enough, her thoughts now are all on Duncan. One of them would have to cast pride to the four winds and make the first move. She will do it, she decides. She'll call him first thing in the morning.

"Muriella?"

Bernie's voice seems to come to her from a great distance. "I'll get you a blanket," she says.

"Stay here beside me. Just a little while. Talk to me. It's still early."

"I'm tired, Bernie."

"Please?"

"I'm really exhausted. I'll be right back."

She pads barefoot into her bedroom and takes a blue blanket from the shelf in her closet.

"Here," she says, throwing it down to him.

He grabs her wrist. "Kiss me goodnight."

She sinks down on the edge of the sofa. "Bernie," she begins, "what happened, happened. We can't change that. But we can't let it go any further. We made a mistake. The best thing to do now is just forget it and move on. I have a man in my life, the only man for me. We had a silly quarrel but I'm going to call him tomorrow."

"You mean you don't want to see me again?"

"Only in class."

"You can't mean that. I love you, Muriella."

"You're too young to know what love is. You're being silly, Bernie."

She knows she's made a mistake as soon as the words leave her mouth. Like lightning, he jumps up, grasps her by the neck, and holds fast. His small hands are surprisingly strong. Unbelievably strong. Then the door to her apartment is thrown open and Duncan is striding towards them.

"He followed me here," she begins, but Duncan will have none of it. "Here's your key," he says, tossing it towards her. "I won't be needing it again." He turns to the boy. "Get dressed, kid. I'll run you home."

As the door slams behind them, Muriella sinks back on the sofa. She stares at the painting of the nude woman in the roses, stares at it until the colours disappear in a blur of tears.

A City Slicker
Goes Hunting

I was a ten-year old tomboy when my parents played host to a young man from Toronto. Mid-winter visits to Manitoulin Island are not for the faint of heart.

His first name was Louis, and he complained loud and long about the lack of entertainment. He couldn't understand how my parents could have forsaken the city for what he called a "howling wilderness of snow".

"You could always go hunting," my dad suggested.

Lou confessed he'd never been hunting, had never, in fact, even held a gun.

"Always a first time for everything," replied Dad. "Maybe you'll have beginner's luck and bag a rabbit. You can use the shotgun I borrowed from Andy Coe."

My father gave Lou a quick lesson in loading and aiming the gun, and, after getting permission to tag along, Lou and I dressed warmly for the great outdoors.

"I'd go with you," said my dad, "but we've asked friends in for a few hands of euchre. Don't pull out a white hankie in the bush," he cautioned. "If there's a Yankee hunter within a mile, he'll think it's a deer and start firing."

White-topped cedars and crusty snowdrifts surrounded us as Lou and I set off into the woods. We saw a lot of different tracks, but they always disappeared after we'd followed them for awhile. Once, we caught sight of a white jackrabbit. Lou fired but missed. Even though I liked rabbit stew, I was glad.

When we came to a cedar fence, Lou stuck the barrel of the gun into the snow and we climbed up to sit on the top rail for a rest. Some time later, another rabbit appeared. Lou lifted the rifle and took a shot at it. He missed again, and the explosion knocked him right off the fence.

"Are you all right?" I asked from my perch at the other end of the rail.

Lou stood up and began brushing off the white flakes that covered him from head to foot. "I think so, kid," he replied. "I don't know what the heck happened."

He walked over to retrieve the gun from the snowbank. The end of the barrel curved downwards as though it had started to melt. Lou shook his head as he looked at it.

Silently, we headed back to the house.

"Good Lord!" my father exclaimed when he saw the gun. "What did you do, Lou, pack the end of the barrel with snow?"

"Maybe you can fix it," Lou replied. "Saw off the end so nobody can tell …"

"Lou, I'd like you to meet our euchre partners," said my mother. "Mr. and Mrs. Andy Coe." Lou turned as red as the mackintosh he was wearing. "I'll make you out a cheque for the gun," he said.

Madame Sylvia's
Prediction

Lisa and Mark Adams should have been having the time of their lives. They could look forward to two whole weeks in glorious Barbados, island of flying fish, coral reefs, and scores of the bearded fig trees for which it was named. A blue and green paradise.

After the honeymooners had left their hotel on the sunny Caribbean beach to prowl around Pelican Village earlier, Lisa had shopped till they were both ready to drop, Mark carrying most of the bags without complaint. Then she'd spotted Madame Sylvia's sign, and the disagreement started, neither of them willing to back down. Now the argument was escalating into a full-blown war of words.

"Why can't this discussion wait till we have lunch?" Mark demands. "Let's try this place. I'm hungry."

"You're always hungry."

He tries to get her to smile. "I'm a growing boy."

Lisa remains silent while he orders their drinks. "I don't really believe in fortune tellers," she finally explains. "I just thought it would be fun to see this one … to ask her a few questions about our future. After all, Mark, what harm could that do?"

"Lots of harm. My mother once went to a palm reader. The woman told her she'd have a serious accident. Two days later my mom fell down the cellar stairs and broke her leg. I think she was following a self-fulfilling prophesy in some strange way. I just think it's a bad idea." He pauses for breath. "A very bad idea."

Lisa studies him over hands clasped tightly together.

"Next thing you'll be running around consulting teacup readers," he continues.

"Madame Sylvia is not a teacup reader. She reads tarot cards. There are seventy-eight cards and each one is different. It's more scientific. Lots of people …"

"Hogwash," he interrupts, "that's what it is. Absolute rubbish. The future's not ours to see."

The waiter sets their calypso flips on the table. "You know Madame Sylvia?" he asks. "I hear you talking about her."

Mark glances up, surprised. "Why do you ask?"

The elderly Barbadian moves closer. "Madame Sylvia turn over cards and speak truth," he says, almost whispering the words.

"What makes you think so?" Lisa enquires.

The waiter looks fearfully around the restaurant before answering. Then he begins in a low voice. "Many years ago, she tell cards for young man from Bathsheba. She tell him he will become murderer on certain day."

"That's bizarre," says Mark. "What happened?" He laughs as he adds, "Did he take a gun and shoot somebody?"

"Young man smile at prediction," says the waiter. "Just like you smile now. Then he decide better not take chance. He make up mind he not leave house on day named. This way, prediction can not come to pass. Night before, he tell friends he go away for whole day so no one come to call on him."

The elderly West Indian lapses into silence, his liquid brown eyes staring past them into a distance only he can see.

"So what happened?" prompts Lisa.

"He go to bed to await fateful day. Morning come, but he not rise. Stay in bed to make time pass. Noon come and he begin to feel thirsty. He get up and punch hole in coconut. He sit by open window, about to drink coconut milk. Is warm day, nice breeze. He angry because he afraid to go out. He want to visit girlfriend in Jericho, but he afraid of prediction."

From outside their restaurant comes the far-off cries of a woman selling drink made from the bark of a mauby tree, her voice sweet and musical on the sunlit air. "Mauby coo-oo-oo, mauby coo-oo-oo."

"What's the rest of the story," Mark urges, forgetting his drink.

"Young man not know then, but he sit holding future in hands."

"How's that?"

"Future in hands," repeats the waiter. "In fit of temper for not go out, he all sudden hurl coconut out open window. He hurl it with all his might. It hit man passing by at time. Hit hard. Man die one hour later. He murderer now. Prediction come true."

"But surely it would be called an accident!" Lisa protests.

"Not so. Turns out fellow he kill is bitter rival for girl in Jericho. Jury say he kill on purpose. He found guilty."

"That's some story," says Mark. "Are you sure you didn't just make it up? Do we have to pay extra for entertainment tax?" he adds, chuckling at his own joke.

"You want order now?" the waiter asks, eyes downcast.

Lisa looks at the menu. "Couscouscu," she reads aloud. "What is it?"

"Dish made from baobab leaves, millet flour, meat. Many visitors like very much."

"We'll try it," says Mark. "And please bring us an order of oysters."

As soon as they are alone, Lisa tosses back her mane of sun-bleached hair and smiles. "What do you think of Madame Sylvia's powers now?" she demands.

A wide grin spreads across Mark's tanned face. "You don't think for one minute I bought that wild story, do you? Come on, Lisa. Flying coconuts! Get real."

"It sounded genuine to me, Mark."

"You're so gullible. He's probably Madame Sylvia's brother helping her drum up business."

"I don't know. Maybe some people do have a gift for prophesy. Madame Sylvia might be one of them."

"Rubbish, Lisa. Anyway, why all this curiosity about the future? What will be, will be."

"I'd still like to see her," she insists. "It said on her sign you have to make an appointment. I want to do it, Mark. Just for fun, Maybe she can tell me how many children we'll have. And whether we'll have girls or boys. Or both, if we're lucky."

"I'd much rather you didn't. But I guess my wishes don't count when it comes to something you're set on doing. I don't know why you're being so stubborn about this."

They finish their meal in an icy silence neither is willing to break.

* * *

Mark gives in as they leave the restaurant. "You win, Lisa," he says. "Do what you want about Madame Sylvia. I won't argue any more. After all, this business isn't worth spoiling our honeymoon over. But let's have a swim before we do anything else. We need to cool off."

"Sounds good to me. I can't wait to show you my new red bikini."

The desk clerk at their hotel smiles as he hands them their key. "Did you have a nice morning at the Village?" he enquires.

"Great," replies Lisa. "We had lunch at *The Pelican*. One of the waiters there told us the strangest story, incredible, really."

"An older man? Sort of sad looking?"

"Why, yes. Do you know him?"

"Only by reputation. He's just been paroled after spending thirty years in prison for murder. A weird case. Seems he threw a coconut at a rival and killed him."

Lisa turns to Mark as they head for their room. "You don't need to say a word," she cautions. "I'm not planning to go anywhere near any fortune tellers. Not now. Not ever."

He gives her a hug, and they move on arm in arm toward their unknown future.

The Fishing Trip

The sun was just rising when we arrived in Paris. Typical early morning in small town Ontario. And yet not typical at all. Special. I knew then that I would remember always the uniqueness of this day. Not that anything really surprising happened. Memory is a strange business at best. Out of the multitude of daily happenings why are there certain days, even certain moments, that we never forget? If we're very lucky we know when they're occurring that we will never forget them.

My father, my uncle and I seemed to be the only people in Paris who were up and about. I had never visited the town before, and I was much taken with its hilly greenery as Uncle Bill drove up the main street and parked in front of what seemed to be the only restaurant open. The three of us went in to order breakfast.

The fast food in that greasy spoon tasted absolutely delicious. Home fries, ham and eggs liberally splashed with ketchup. Piles of buttered brown toast. We needed a hearty breakfast. We were on our way to a farm to pick up spears to go fishing in a stream a mile or so behind the farmhouse. Uncle Bill knew the family and they were expecting us. I wasn't giving any thought at the time as to the legality of spear fishing. I had a hunch that my uncle was exercising the prerogative of some of his ancestors, but he was my uncle by marriage only, and I had never had a chance to ask him. He dropped out of our lives shortly after that day when he and my aunt decided to go their separate ways. My dad and I had never even thought about spear fishing before, let alone trying it. But the idea smacked of adventure, and that was enough. As an extra bonus for me, it was a day away from housework and children, thanks to a willing husband.

We all had seconds of the strong black coffee. There was no need to hurry. The day stretched ahead of us, misty and unending.

Finally, the men slid some silver under their saucers, paid the bill, and we were on our way.

Even after all these years, I still recall the wacky conviviality of the people who lived on that farm. They were a large, boisterous family with a number of very large teenagers. Good spirits abounded; an egg-throwing contest was in full swing when we entered the huge, old-fashioned kitchen. Eggs were flying back and forth like so many white and brown birds. I surprised myself by catching the one that came hurtling towards me.

Before we left to try our luck, one of the teens asked if I was my dad's wife. He was so pleased I had no desire to spoil the moment for him by acting insulted. Anyway, with my well-scrubbed face, denim overalls, and rubber boots I was looking anything but young and glamorous.

The sun was climbing higher and the air growing warmer as we set off across the muddy fields behind the house. Our husky farmer-guide set a brisk pace, but we had no trouble keeping up with him.

The stream was clear and cold; we followed it for what seemed like miles as it wound an erratic course across the countryside. There's something about holding a spear in one hand with the idea of catching food that brings out atavistic instincts. We didn't talk. It was enough just to be wading along, enjoying the sun and the sounds of the rushing water.

It was the most successful fishing trip I ever took. And we didn't even see a single fish.

Decision In Bangkok

Caitlin frowned at Victor across a huge bouquet of ginger flowers in the lobby of the Royal River Hotel. Her mother's words came back to her. "Travelling together before marriage is a good idea. They say it's the acid test of a relationship."

"I'm flunking the test," Caitlin said to herself. It started right at the airport when Victor had left behind the magazine he'd borrowed from her, a half-finished crossword puzzle inside.

"You get upset over nothing," he observed now, his cool manner driving her crazy. "If you wanted everything to be the same as it was at home, we should have stayed there."

"All I'm saying is if you'd moved your butt we could have caught the eight o'clock shuttle boat and done some sight-seeing before it gets too hot. Now we're stuck here for an hour."

"Quit whining, my love."

"I am not whining. I never whine."

"Let's go for a walk," he suggested, adding with a chuckle, "to cool off."

Just as they reached the entrance, a curtain of rain descended without warning, dimpling the brown surface of the Chao Phraya, the River of Kings.

"See how lucky we are," Victor remarked. "Let's go have another coffee."

"I'm glad it didn't rain for our river cruise last night. It would have spoiled everything."

Victor's shining brown eyes, she decided, were the exact colour of the coffee the waiter placed before them. It was his eyes that had first attracted her, a legacy from his Jamaican mother. She should relax, she told herself. Roll with the punches. Stop getting upset over Vic's untidiness, telephones that wouldn't work, heat that was unrelenting. She'd known it would be hot, but she'd wanted to visit Thailand ever since seeing *The King and I* as a child. Summer was the only time she and Vic could get away before the fall. They'd met in the high school where they both taught, she English and he math, her worst subject all through school.

They really didn't have much in common. But they were in love. Was that going to be enough?

"A *baht* for your thoughts," he said. "That's about four times more than a penny, so you're getting a good price."

"I was thinking it's a good thing we're with a tour or I'd never get you anywhere on time. It's supposed to be women who are always late." She softened her words with a smile, unwilling to start another argument. Perhaps she was just over-tired. They'd had an early start yesterday to visit the Temple, the *Wat Pra Kaew,* to see the famous Emerald Buddha. Even early in the morning, it had been a perishing 35 degrees centigrade. She'd imagined all the gold melting off all the *stupas.* They'd had to take off their shoes before entering the shrine. She'd gladly have taken off everything but her Tilley hat, her silly hat, Vic called it.

Inside the temple, a sign directed visitors to refrain from pointing their bare feet toward the most sacred image for Buddhists. The whole compound of the Grand Palace had surpassed even her high expectations. Mother-of-pearl throne, exquisite murals, inlaid jewels and mirrors, it was breathtaking. A city of gilt and gold, a storybook come alive. Caitlin and the King of Siam. Who was it now, Rama the Ninth?

Victor broke into her reverie. "We don't have to wait for the boat. Let's take a bus. It's our free time. Let's be adventurous."

He paid the cheque and they made their way out of the dining room, passing a large tank in the lobby where two sharks swam around in endless circles.

The traffic was horrendous. Pink taxis everywhere. Scores of Toyotas, Isuzus, and Nissans. At one point she saw an open truck carrying pigs crowded together with two young men. A great deal of construction was going on — roads, houses, shopping malls, viaducts. Caitlin was fascinated with the ubiquitous spirit houses — small scale temples Thais placed in their front yards so departed loved ones would have a place to come to. They were the size of children's play houses and very colourful. She wished she could take one home.

"Let's price them just for fun," said Victor.

"Remember," she reminded him, "we have to be back at the hotel by five-thirty sharp to go to the *Piman Thai Theatre* for dinner."

"Don't worry so much. Let's just have fun."

Have fun they did, shopping, taking pictures, soaking up city scenes, and doing their best to ignore the heat. They even managed to make it back to their hotel in time for a refreshing swim before dressing for dinner. Maybe the teachers were going to pass her mother's "travel test" after all, Caitlin reflected.

The other thirty-seven members of their tour group were mostly women. With his ready laugh and dark good looks, Victor made a big hit with them. Caitlin was glad she wasn't the jealous type.

* * *

Bangkok by night was a fairyland of trees decorated with little white lights. Perfect for lovers, she thought, though she could have done without the 711 Variety Store, Pizza Hut, and Macdonald's. No escaping some sights, she reflected, noting a few street people sleeping beneath a viaduct.

When they were seated at low tables, several waiters hurried in with an array of individual dishes: rice noodles in a broth with fish, grilled chicken, meat balls with chili sauce, all bearing names she couldn't begin to pronounce. Something for every taste bud — sweet, sour, salty, and hot. "Beware of that red sauce," Vic warned. "It's a killer."

As soon as the first dancers appeared, scores of smokers lit up. Caitlin's eyes were smarting from the fumes.

"We should have brought some durian for dessert to get even," Victor whispered in her ear.

She laughed, recalling the delicious taste of the creamy white fruit that could only be eaten by holding one's nose at the same time. They'd tried it in their hotel room. It smelled worse than goat droppings. She'd brushed her teeth for a good twenty minutes. Victor had wrapped the big pits in three plastic bags to keep the stench from escaping.

The *gamelan* orchestra accompanying the dancers sounded like a dozen xylophones. Caitlin marvelled at the way the girls could bend their hands back into swan shapes. She'd read that Thai girls started training for this art at the age of six. In some of the numbers the dancers smiled, in others they remained totally expressionless. Finally, the last dancer appeared, her classic good looks a picture postcard, a slim golden beauty with long, pearly fingernails and bright red lips. "Isn't she the pret ...," Caitlin began.

Without moving his eyes from the dancer, Victor put his index finger to his lips. He seemed completely mesmerized. Caitlin felt an unfamiliar pang she recognized as jealousy. Though she chided herself for being so foolish, she felt hurt. She hated being shushed.

"*Suay*," he breathed when the performance was over. "*Suay*."

"Yes, beautiful," she agreed, her words coated with ice.

He didn't even notice her pique. The day that had been so good — *dee* in Thai, was now *mai dee*. Just as Victor had changed the day for her, putting *mai* in front of a word changed it to the opposite meaning.

Back at the hotel, the usual orchids decorated their pillows. She was glad they had twin beds. Staying angry in a double bed would have been next to impossible.

"I'm tired," she protested when he made a move to join her under the sheets. "I just want to sleep."

It took her ages to drift off. His gentle snore infuriated her. "Let's get married at the end of August," he'd urged, "just before school starts. She'd agreed at the time. Now she was drowning in doubt. Everything was "let's" with Victor. Let's do this, let's do that. He made life seem so simple. But it wasn't. How was a person to choose a lifetime mate wisely? Victor was an only child. Perhaps his mother had spoiled him, picked up after him all the time. His parents argued a lot, but they always patched things up. They were soon to celebrate their thirty-first anniversary. Her parents had never fought, yet they had come to a parting of the ways after twenty-six years of marriage. An amicable parting, but painful for Caitlin and her sister even though they were both on their own.

* * *

At some point in the early dawn, she felt him slip into bed beside her, whispering words of love, putting one leg over her. Her resolve to stay aloof fled like dry leaves before a strong wind.

Afterwards, they had to rush like crazy to get down to the lobby so they could have breakfast before catching their coach to visit Kanchanaburi province and the River Kwai. They went first to the rickety old wooden JEATH Museum. Pong, their guide, said the letters stood for Japan, England, America, Australia, Taiwan, and Holland. They studied dozens of yellowed newspaper pictures and articles from the 40s about the building of the railway across the River Kwai so Japan would have a faster route to China. Thousands of prisoners of war died, as well as many Thais pressed into working on the project.

"My grandfather told me about this place," said Victor. "There was a Doctor Dunlop from Australia who was a big hero to the men in keeping up their spirits."

"Some of these clippings are about him," said Caitlin. "It must have been horrible working in this heat with nothing much to eat except rice and salt. No wonder so many died of cholera and dysentery."

She moved away from him to write a few words in the Visitors' Book.

They ate lunch at the *Tham Krasae Camp* restaurant. Scads of flies tried to get between them and their plates of spaghetti. "What time do we get the train?" asked Victor.

"One o'clock," she replied, unwrapping a piece of sugarless gum. It had melted in the heat.

The train was half an hour late. Victor, his customary good humour undiminished, had started a 'train dance', much to the delight of the group. When he beckoned her to join in, she declared she was too hot to move.

At last, they boarded. The train's hard wooden seats were painted a rusty brown colour. Caitlin grabbed the first empty one, and Victor sat down beside her. Across the aisle from them, a young, tattooed Thai took out a small brown bottle from his shirt pocket and sniffed something up each nostril. He continued to do this as the train rattled along. He looked sleepier each time. Finally, he passed out, his feet sticking out in the aisle. Passengers had to step over him to get off at their stations. An elderly woman with a large basket sat facing them. She was chewing betel nut, her decayed teeth making her look as though she had a mouthful of blood.

The scenery through the wide open window was fascinating. Hills that looked like paintings she'd seen of Chinese mountains. Two huge working elephants at one station. Stands of lush palm trees. Glimpses of village life.

Pong gave the signal and they detrained right at the site of the bridge over the River Kwai. Vic turned to her. "Know something strange? Back at the museum, I wrote 'Very moving, such tragic times' in the Visitors' Book. Then I looked up to see what some of the others in our group had written, and you'd put down the very same words."

Caitlin had no time to reply. Their guide was herding them toward longboats. They were taken in sets of six on an exciting trip along the river, the Thai boatmen racing each other to create a wonderful cooling breeze mixed with a fine spray.

When they were on their way back to the hotel, the coach driver took them to *Nakorn Pathon* to see the tallest pagoda in the world — a giant *stupa* of orange-coloured brick with forty-six marble steps leading up to the first part, where a standing golden Buddha stared benignly down as worshippers presented lotus blossoms and the all-pervasive incense sticks.

One more day, thought Caitlin. If our last day here is half as good as this, we'll be doing the wedding march in August. Her flame of hope was as bright as the red and yellow flowers of the flamboyant peacock trees.

* * *

Their last day in Bangkok began with the usual problem of getting Victor moving. "Haul ass!" she finally shouted, "or we'll be left behind."

"Oh, teach," he teased, "if your English students could hear you now."

When they sat down in the coach, the last to board, she realized she'd forgotten her camera. She blamed him, and they started the morning with a quarrel. She'd been looking forward to this trip to the Floating Market at *Damnoen Saduak*, sixty kilometres away. Now the day was ruined. She would have no pictures to take home.

A couple of hours later, they were being packed like sardines into a boat. A Thai girl snapped their picture just before they departed.

As they sped along, Caitlin reached down to touch the water. Victor pulled her arm back. Then she recalled they'd been told to keep their hands and feet well inside the boat to avoid losing pieces of them.

Though the great outboard motors made enough noise to warn of their presence, it still seemed to Caitlin an invasion of privacy when they passed by close to villagers. The *Chao Phraya* served as front yard for people who lived in wooden shacks on pilings along its banks. Children splashed in the shallows, women soaped laundry in the brown water, and one middle-aged monk was busily pushing up his saffron robe to scratch his thigh.

The canal was a carnival of colours, jammed with canoes loaded with farm produce, boats filled with heaps of bananas, coconuts, lemons, and chili peppers. Little sampans carried charcoal braziers offering for sale deep-fried spring rolls, roasted eggs, fried bananas, and sweet, crisp pancakes. Pungent odours abounded, making Caitlin feel slightly queasy.

Though they could buy just about anything under the sun at the Floating Market, Caitlin wanted only a Coke.

Mangy, hungry-looking dogs roamed about. Two of them began to fight, but an old man struck the aggressive one with a big stick, and that was the end of hostilities.

"That's the kind of referee we need," joked Victor.

Caitlin couldn't help laughing, and for awhile her traveller's grouchiness subsided.

It surfaced again when they were almost ready to board their coach to go for lunch at The Rose Gardens. There, all the photographs taken when they'd set out were pressed on cheap white plates, displayed for sale. After searching for a few minutes, they found theirs. "It's terrible of me," she said. "I don't want it."

"It's only a few hundred *bahts*. It'll be a great souvenir. I'm going to get it."

"Please yourself," she retorted, adding under her breath, "you always do."

The show following lunch provided enthralling entertainment: Thai Boxing, Fingernail Dance, Sword Fight, Wedding Ceremony, Bamboo Dance. Caitlin kept wishing she had her camera.

Things came to a head that evening when they were packing for home.

"Get your junk off my side of the dresser," Caitlin cried. "How am I supposed to get organized with a mess like this?" With one arm, she pushed his purchases aside. The souvenir picture plate toppled to the floor, broke neatly in half, and separated his smiling face from her frowning one. She stared down at it, dumbstruck. It was like an omen. She turned and fled into the bathroom, locking the door behind her.

Later, when she emerged from a warm bath that did nothing to relax her, he was gone. The room was tidy. He'd done his packing. She was overwhelmed with despair. She'd been a nit-picking bitch and now she'd lost him. So what if he left the toilet seat up or the toothpaste uncapped? Those weren't character flaws. He was so easy going, so much fun to be with. And good-hearted. She'd known at the time he'd only bought the photo plate because the poor young Thai girl was so anxious to sell it. She didn't know what had gotten into her. She couldn't blame the heat for her last outburst. Their room was air-conditioned.

Clutching the bath towel around her, she sank down on Vic's bed.

A few moments later, he entered with a "Ta, Dah!" fanfare, bearing aloft the mended plate. "They gave me some glue in the kitchen," he explained, "and I patched it up. Look. You can hardly see where it was broken. We're together again."

Caitlin rose, dropping her towel to hold him close. They would sometimes have rough sailing, she knew, but they would always be able to patch things up.

One Too Many

The scene in the child's bedroom is the worst. The upper part of the boy's body is covered in blood, his curly brown hair matted with it, but he's still alive. He's wearing pale blue pyjamas with space ship designs. Across the hall, in the master bedroom, the woman, most likely his mother, is beyond help. Ed Jackson has seen a lot in his fifteen years on homicide; he doesn't understand why he's falling apart now. Maybe, he thinks, it's that — what do you call it? — cumulative effect. Everything in the child's room looks larger than life — the boy's body, his bed, his dresser, the model airplane, the bloody hammer — especially the hammer. It looks huge to him.

"Where the hell's that ambulance?" Ed demands as his partner joins him in the child's room. "It should be here. What's keeping them?"

"It's coming now," Rick replies. "You gone deaf, Eddie?"

Ed realizes he hasn't heard the siren. He needs help, he thinks. But he can't let on. Police officers have to be tough. He has a job to do. He looks down at the boy. He's still breathing. So young. About the same age as his twins, he figures. He can't wait for this day to end, can't wait to get home.

When finally they've filed their reports and the two officers are leaving the station, Rick turns to him. "Don't make the same mistakes I did, Ed," he advises. "Don't take it home with you."

"I won't. I'm just sorry they couldn't save the boy. I thought he had a chance. Jeez, I hope we nab that father of his. I'm pretty sure he's the one who made the 911 call. I don't know why, Rick, but I can't seem to get those images out of my mind. I can't stop thinking about that kid. He was about the same age as my boys."

"Yeah. Damn shame. Wanna go for a drink? Might help."

"I'd better not. Way I feel right now, I'd start drinking and never stop. Besides, my wife will be waiting for me."

"Yeah, lucky you. See you tomorrow then."

Ed decides to walk the eight blocks to his house. He needs time to think, time to clear his head. Rick's words run through his mind. "Don't take it home."

Good advice. Rick learned the hard way. His wife took their daughter and left him a couple of years ago after he had one drink too many and lost his temper once too often. Ed recalls Rick telling him that his ex always seemed to be nagging him about something or other. Usually something minor. His partner's complaints come back to him now. How the hell was he supposed to get worked up over a broken fingernail, Rick had demanded, or even a broken washing machine, after some of the things they had to cope with in Homicide? Good question, Ed had agreed. But Rick shouldn't have taken it out on his wife. His partner hardly ever sees his daughter now. Claims he doesn't know how to talk to a teenage girl. He confides in Ed when he's been drinking, and he's drinking a lot lately. Maybe, Ed muses, I'd be hitting the bottle too if I lost my family. He couldn't even begin to imagine a life without Tina and the boys. They were his lifeline, his island of sanity in a world that often seemed sordid beyond belief.

As he walks, Ed keeps re-living the murder scene. He feels certain it will turn out to be the husband who's guilty. It almost always is the one closest to the victims in cases like these. From time to time, Ed's eyes well up with tears, despite his best efforts to stop them. Maybe he's seen too many scenes of domestic violence. Maybe one too many … He's still choking back sobs when he nears his small brick bungalow. He tries hard to get a grip on himself. Last thing he wants to do is upset Tina or his boys. He tries to compose his features into something approaching a smile.

His eight-year-old twins are riding their new red birthday bikes in front of the house. They jump off them and run to meet him, both of them talking at once. Far from being identical, the two boys even have different coloured hair. Tommy's blonde like him, while Teddy's like his mother. He has curly brown hair — hair like the boy that … Ed pushes the picture from his mind and clasps his sons in a three-way hug.

"You're holding us too tight, Dad," Teddy complains.

"Yeah, you're crushing us to pieces," Tommy agrees.

Reluctantly, Ed frees them. "What's for dinner?" he asks.

"Beef stew," they reply in unison. "Yuck!"

Ed comes close to smiling as they go back to their bikes. He finds Tina getting ready to set the table in the dining room. She shakes out a large white tablecloth and holds it in front of her as she looks up at him, brown eyes shining a welcome. He has a sudden flashback of the murdered woman sprawled on her blood-soaked bed in the master bedroom of the house on Steel Avenue. She had long chestnut coloured hair — just like Tina's. Ed feels his eyes well up again. He shakes his head in an effort to dispel the horrific vision. He really is losing it, he thinks. Maybe he'll have to ask to see a psychologist. But what would that do to his macho image? Everybody at the station thinks of him as Big Ed — the strong man. The man who can deal with anything that comes his way.

"Hungry?" Tina asks.

He stares at her without answering, still fighting the unwelcome images of the murder scene.

"You look tired," she says. "Supper's almost ready. It's not the boys' favourite, but …"

All at once Teddy comes racing into the room, his brother close behind him. "I fell off my bike, Mom," he shouts. "I fell because Tommy ran into me! It's all his fault!" The boy holds up a scraped elbow for her inspection and begins to howl. His twin joins him, protesting his innocence.

"Stop that awful racket this minute!" Tina admonishes them. *"Big boys don't cry."*

Ed looks from his son's bloody elbow to his wife's stern young face. He takes a deep breath and forces himself to remain calm and speak quietly. "Yes, Tina, they do. Sometimes big boys do cry." Then he goes to get their first-aid kit from the bathroom.

Bye Baby Bunting

On Friday night Grace returned home late from her restaurant job, bone-weary and ready for bed. She'd stayed an extra half hour to clean up some sugar she'd spilled. She wasn't one to leave a mess behind for somebody else to worry about.

Grace heard voices as she turned her key in the lock. One of them sounded like Donald's. She froze. Several seconds passed before she could bring herself to enter the foyer of her dingy third-floor apartment. The smell of cigarette smoke engulfed her, and she stood still, listening.

"You agree the bastard's gotta get it. Question is, how?"

Grace's breath caught in her throat. It *was* Donald's voice. After years of not hearing from him, not wanting to hear from him.

"Let's get Jake to rig up one of his bombs," came a deeper voice.

"Naw. We wanna see Fat Sam's face when we give it to him. Hey — think of all that lard when he starts to shake. Christ! I hate fat slobs. I gotta say one thing fer my old man. He never let hisself get fat."

"Beating you up must of kept him in shape."

At the high-pitched sound of their laughter, Grace stole forward and peeked into her living room. A young girl lay sprawled on the beige sofa, breasts jiggling under a tight red sweater.

"We'll use a knife," Donald said. "That's quick and easy and we can scare the shit out of him first."

The other man showed a row of tobacco-stained teeth as he grinned his approval. "Let me do it, okay, Don?"

"Yeah," agreed the girl. "Let Gil do it."

"Nope. I got a better idea. We all do it. We give it to Fat Sam just like Julius Caesar got it."

Grace ducked back out of sight. A sudden memory of Donald as a baby brought stinging tears. Laying there in the crook of her arms, staring up at her with them puzzled brown eyes. Then a spunky little toddler, so cute with his big smile and thick, dark curls. *Bye Baby Bunting*, she used to croon to him. Then

Donald growing up … changing. Reluctantly, Grace turned her attention back to the conversation. The man called Gil was talking.

"We still got to decide where and when …" His words came to a dead stop as he caught sight of Grace.

"Don't panic," Donald drawled as he lit a cigarette. "It's only my ole lady. How are ya, Ma?" Without waiting for an answer, he turned back to his buddy. "We'll get him right in his ole cigar store. When the guys get out next week, we'll meet there … just before closing time. Hey — that'll be March 15th. Perfect! Beware the Ides of March, you big-mouthed old kike."

"Beware the *ideas* of Donald," parroted Gil.

The girl looked puzzled, but she joined in their laughter, ignoring Grace. Her long, straight hair fell like brown drapes over her small, pinched face as she struggled up to a sitting position.

Grace found her voice. "What are you people doing here?" she demanded. "What do you want?"

"We need a place to hide out for a couple of days, Ma. Seems this guy from the Choppers decided to commit suicide." He grinned. "He done it by crucifying hisself."

The three of them seemed about to choke with amusement.

Grace took a step forward. "I want you all out of here. You're no son of mine, Donald. Not as long as you wear that Blood Brothers jacket."

"Come on, Ma. It's only a couple of days. You stay outta our hair, we'll stay outta yers."

Grace's eyes took in the revolver tossed carelessly with several comic books on top of her walnut coffee table which was overflowing with china saucers used as ashtrays and empty beer cans. "Get out!" she shouted. "You think you can come in here and talk about killing poor old Sam Cohen, a man we know, a man who aint never hurt …"

Gill interrupted her. "That poor man you're defending insulted your son, lady. Nobody insults a Blood Brother and lives."

Donald tugged as his shaggy black beard. "Fuck, yeah. Nobody insults a Blood Brother. He'll never throw any of us outta his crummy store again. You can bet yer ass on that."

Grace took off her coat. "If you don't leave now, I'm calling the police."

Donald turned to his friends. "You 'n Shirl go down to the corner and get us some eats — chips or something. Pizza maybe. Lotsa cheese. Time you get back, I'll have her straightened out."

Gil loped toward the door and the girl followed, moving cat-like in her tight blue jeans.

"Hey — turn them jackets inside out," Donald warned. "Don't want any Choppers seeing our double Bs. Not till the Brothers get here next week. They'll see more'n they wanna see of us then."

Grace went to hang up her gray spring coat. When she returned, she sank down on an easy chair facing her son. "Donald, you're twenty-eight years old. Why can't you get a regular job … settle down."

"Hey — I'm doing okay, Ma. Better than okay. You oughta see my new bike. Christ! I'm telling you, it's really something."

"Donny, you've got to get out of this club before it's too late. You're in for nothing but trouble, believe me."

"It's a real beauty, Ma, my new bike. I could put it right here in the living room and be happy just to sit and look at it. Bright red, lotsa chrome, damn near any extra you could think of. Kind I used to dream of having when I was twelve."

"You was such a cute little boy, Donny. Whenever your father was off on one of his binges, I used to sing to you: *Bye Baby Bunting, Daddy's gone a hunting* … and you'd look up at me, your eyes big as saucers. You had scads of dark curls … soft … like my hair used to be. You was such a happy little boy …"

"I'm not a little boy any more, Ma, so quit the crap."

"Get out of this club, Donald. For my sake. I'm begging you."

"Once a Brother, always a Brother, that's our motto. We're hard on them that leave."

"What do you do to them?"

"Stomp on them. Squash them."

"And you think that's all right?"

"It's our rules."

"If everybody had them kind of rules, what would the world be like?"

"Great. Exciting."

"Donald, I can't talk to you no more. I aint been able to talk to you for years."

"You don't get it, Ma. We're special. Us Blood Brothers aint like ninety percent of the rest of the people. We're one percenters. We live by our own ten commandments — thou *shall* commit adultery, thou *shall* steal, thou *shall* kill any son of a bitch that gets in our way. Or insults us."

Grace looked down at her hands. They were red — dark red from the new detergent they were using in the diner. Blood red. She shuddered.

Donald popped open a can of beer and flopped down on the beige sofa. "Maybe we'll go after somebody really big next time," he mused aloud. "Somebody really important. When guys like us that never went to university or nothing can bring down the big guys, man, that's power."

"You're worse than your father, Donald. I'm sorry I gave birth to you. You're a bad seed."

"Speaking of the old man, did he ever come back?"

"Never."

"You shouldn't of took my part against him."

"I was afraid he'd kill you."

"Fat chance. I'd of took him first."

"We do what we have to do," Grace murmured. "Whatever seems right to us at the time."

"Chrissake, Ma, that's what I been trying to tell you. So get off my back!"

Grace stared at him across the lifetime of the untidy room, a room that seemed no longer familiar. She didn't see the black beard covering half her son's face, the beer can in his hand, the twisted line of his mouth. She saw only the dark, brown eyes and now they were baby's eyes, shiny and big. He was looking up at her from the crook of her arm in the General Hospital … staring up at her …

Grace leaned forward and picked up the gun from the coffee table.

"Hey — don't play with that …" Donald began.

When she pointed it, he lunged at her.

For a long time, Grace couldn't remember anything that happened that day. They told her she had called the police herself. Told her she was cradling Donald's head in her arms and singing something that sounded like a lullaby when they found her.

Even though the kitchen in her new apartment was filled with August heat, Grace shivered. Donald would have been thirty-five years old last Thursday, she thought, the very day of her release from prison. She dried her supper dishes, then wiped the coral counter top until it shone. After wringing out the dishcloth, she folded it with care and hung it over the taps in the sink to dry. She was eager to go back out to her balcony, to breathe more free air. Free after seven long years. She could thank the good people on the parole board for that. On a bread and butter plate, she carried with her a thick slab of watermelon. Sheer luxury.

The sun was low when Grace folded her aluminum chair and set it against the railing of her balcony. Before going inside, she noticed several dark brown watermelon seeds she'd dropped on the green outdoor carpeting. She stooped down to pick up every single one of them. It wouldn't do to leave a mess behind.

Her Lucky Day

On the last Saturday in September, Nina plodded along the beach, head down, wondering how she was going to eat for the next few days. Being a poor student wasn't a helluva lot of fun. And she still had a whole year to go on her computer programmer's course.

When she spotted the black wallet under some scrubby bushes, she blinked in disbelief. Then she snatched it up. Inside were four credit cards, a SIN card, a health card, and a driver's licence in the name of one Dustin Dempsey. Also, a dental appointment card, a folded in half lottery crossword puzzle, four brown one hundred dollar bills, and two green twenties.

Nina studied the face on the driver's licence. The euphonious name brought a smile to her lips. Dustin Dempsey looked affluent. Anybody who walked around with that much cash deserved to lose it. He probably wouldn't even miss it. She could dump the wallet into the nearest bank and keep the money. She needed it a lot more than he did. Perhaps it was meant to be an answer to her prayers. After all, if she hadn't been so downcast, she wouldn't have seen the wallet at all.

* * *

Nina stared out across the sparkling blue waters of Lake Huron. Then she began to move slowly ahead. Maybe she should do the crossword puzzle. She and her friends bought them once in awhile, but none of them had ever won more than three dollars — the price of the puzzle — for uncovering two complete words. Still, you never could tell.

She sat down on a log, and with a blue-painted thumbnail scratched off the first of the eighteen letters at the top of the card. An R. There were seven of them in the puzzle. A good sign. The letters L,O,F,C,U, and P followed, making her heart beat a little faster each time. When she finished, she had uncovered seven complete words. Excited, she looked at the Prize Legend at the bottom of the card. She'd won a hundred dollars! Three of the words were *four, leaf,* and *clover.* Surely that was a message meant for her alone. A hundred would get her by nicely until her next cheque. Now she could return the wallet, cash and conscience intact. First, though, she would have to replace the puzzle. There was a small variety store just up from the beach. She could get one there and check in the phone book as well. How many Dustin Dempseys could there be in a place this size?

Nina collected her winnings from a bored, teenage clerk, bought a replacement puzzle, and looked in the phone book for her unknown benefactor. He lived on Donegal Drive. The alliteration amused her. His wife's name was probably Debbie. The Dempseys lived within a short walking distance. She decided not to call first. Surprising him might be better. She ought to get a damn good reward.

Clutching the wallet in one hand, Nina stood on the small, driftwood-decorated front veranda waiting for the bell to be answered.

A short, dark haired man, the one pictured on the driver's licence, responded to her summons. He appeared completely mystified as she extended the wallet. In the background, she could hear Saturday's family noises. Probably kids fighting over the TV.

"It's yours," she said. "I found it in the sand."

He opened the wallet and looked inside. "Good Lord! I didn't even know it was missing. It must have fallen out of my pocket when I took my jacket off on the beach this morning. This is so good of you. I can't thank you enough."

"A reward would be nice."

Nina grinned, waiting expectantly.

"Here you are, Miss." He took out the two twenty dollar bills and held them out to her. Nina made no move to take them. "I think I deserve more," she protested. "After all, I could have kept all the cash. I think you should give me one of those brown bills." She attempted a smile that didn't quite come off.

"Young woman, you think you should be paid for being honest?"

"Well ... yes. After all, I could have just kept the money."

"I see. Very well, here you are." He shoved a hundred dollar bill at her and closed the door in her face.

The following Monday, Nina was idly leafing through the daily paper when a small headline in the second section caught her eye. She mouthed the words: Local Man Wins Fifty Thousand in Lottery. Eleven words uncovered for top prize in Instant Crossword Puzzle. Nina sensed what the name would be even before she saw it. It was Dustin Dempsey. It was the card she bought for him. On her lucky day.

Pumpkin Lady

My too-easy smile betrays me again. Too late to kill it, even though it's not being returned. Always been so anxious to please. Pathetically anxious. Should have learned reticence by now. If the years don't bring wisdom, why go on living them out? Seventy-nine autumns I'll have weathered — if I make it through this one. It's hard to keep from being afraid when the leaves begin to fall. Especially this year. This year when I can't rake them up.

Maybe the old fool thought I was trying to vamp him. Just being neighborly … or trying to be. But how can anybody be neighborly in this high-rise beehive? We go unsmiling, each to his private cell. His private hell.

Where the devil is my key? Should never buy a handbag with more than one compartment. Can hear Susan's voice now. *Don't go out without your key, Mother. You know how absent-minded you are these days.*

Good old Susan. Can always count on her for daily reminders of my mental deficiencies. Well with my memory I'd probably forget 'em all if she didn't. I'd probably have tried to struggle along, all alone in the house …

The house. Old, ramshackle place. Knew every nook and cranny of it well as I know the back of my hand. It had lots of trouble spots, sure. Like my hand has liver spots. But it would have worked out. If only they'd given me a chance. Shouldn't say "they". This was Susan's doing. All of it.

Be putting in bulbs if I were home now. Bearded iris and grape hyacinths. And tulips. Lots and lots of tulips. Red and yellow promises of spring. Like the waxy colors my first-grade children used.

Better stop this rambling and find that damned key. Walk wasn't worth all this effort. Nothing but concrete around here anyway. Nothing to walk to. No park. Not like my old neighborhood.

Ah, here it is. First compartment I looked in after all. Better take those glasses out of their case and put them on my head. Never see the key-hole without them. It's not vanity. It's just that they hurt my nose. Susan says it's all in my mind. 'Tisn't though. Fool things feel like a great ugly bird perched on the bridge of my nose. Leave red claw marks for hours. Haven't got a big fat face like

Susan. 'Course she's fat as a pillow all over. Doesn't take after me there. Harry either.

Harry. How many weeks is it now? Never mind. Open the door. There. Good thing I left a light on. Only six-thirty and already dark. Must be about eight weeks. Will be two months exactly on the twenty-eighth of October. Maybe this *is* the twenty-eighth. Hard to tell. Lost all track of time since moving in here. Only a week ago. Seems a lot longer.

'Course they're right, Susan and Paul. They might as well have the money now. Be theirs someday anyway. Someday soon, way I feel tonight. No appetite at all. Always had such a good one when Harry was alive. Somebody to cook for … to share with. Can't be bothered eating. Jus as soon sit here and stare at my Jack o' Lantern. He *does* look a lot like me. Susan said so when I was carving him the other day. Couldn't see it then. But now that the mouth is beginning to droop at the corners. Might as well set my glasses here on the table. I've seen enough.

Ha! Susan accused me of acting like a kid when she caught me in the act of carving you, Jack. Talk about parents not understanding children! Other way around, if you ask me. Why I've carved your likeness every year for as long as I can remember. But you don't look the same in here. You should be in the bay window of my house where you belong. There'll be children again this year. Lots of them. I would have been all right. If they'd just given me a little more time to get used to the idea of being alone.

Why did Paul just stand there and let Susan take over like that? He's the older, after all. Guess he had no time to think. Had to get back to his family in Vancouver. Anyway, with Paul, that was the natural way. Susan always did order him about. Now his bright-eyed wife and daughters do the same. Men's Lib — that's what Paul's always needed. Hope for his sake life *does* begin at forty. He'll soon be there.

Ha! I'm a fine one to talk about liberation. Letting myself be railroaded into moving in here. More like an old folks home than an apartment building. Surrounded by senior citizens. Hate that term. Rather be called "Old Trout". That's what that nice British nurse called me when I had to take therapy for my arm. Shoulder still bothers me sometimes. Susan said I should have known better than to try to rescue a treed cat at my age. Especially when it wasn't even my cat. Couldn't argue with her there. Useless to argue with Susan anyway. She always turns out to be right. Suppose that's why I let her talk me into this move …

Maybe the house won't sell. It's pretty old-fashioned. Maybe nobody'll want it. And there's all our furniture to be disposed of first … funny how I still think "our" and "we" instead of "I". Still can't believe he's really gone. Never forget his face that morning. Thought he was just sleeping in. But when I pulled back the covers … well, maybe that is the best way to go. Everybody says so. Lord, I wish I was back in my old house …

Don't mean to be insulting, Jack, but you're not much of a conversationalist.

Susan always was one to take over. "Great qualities of leadership" her report cards said. Never thought that leadership would be turned against me.

People say such stupid things at funerals. Suppose they're trying to give comfort. May have done the same thing myself. But Mattie Jackson saying, "I always did like that tie on Harry" — that was too much.

Wish you'd quit looking at me like that, Jack. You and your droopy orange cheeks and weak mouth. Carved you too soon this year, that's clear. You're falling apart before your time. Here — maybe if you wear my hat you'll cheer up. No? Well, it fits you about as well as it fits me. In fact, black velvet is just right for you. You look like a regular old Halloween lady. Better call you "Jackie".

Lord, it's dark. That's the worst part of the fall. Gets so dark so early. Cold, too. Should put you out on the balcony, Jackie. The better to save you, my dear. But save you for what? Won't be any trick-or-treaters this year. No goblins allowed here. Or witches, or pirates, or spacemen, or ghosts. Never mind. We'll take you out to the balcony anyway.

Such a spread of lights down there! Can see clear across the river to Port Huron. Just like being in an airplane living way up here. Remote. Cars in the parking lot look like those matchbox toys we used to buy for Paul …

With her head tucked underneath her arm, she walks the bloody tower. Ah, you're in fine voice tonight, Ellie Hunter. Keep this up and they'll be sending for the men in white coats. Might be better off if they did. Madness, like misery, loves company.

We had our miseries too, Harry and I. Lord, some of the fights we had! Wasn't what you could call a smooth marriage. Kids coming along so late in life didn't help matters. But one thing — we were always able to take each other for granted. I liked that, no matter what those so-called marriage counselors say against it. Nothing better in the world than having somebody you can always take for granted. Real security, that. Crime the way so many marriages are breaking up today.

Sure didn't think he'd be the one to go first. Two years younger than me and all. How he used to razz me about that! Bothered me no end when we were first married. Lots of things bothered me then. Always wanted everything just so. Always too damned anxious to please. Wanted to be liked, I guess. Not sure I ever was though.

Wouldn't be much left of a person if she were to fall from this height. Nothing but a lump on the parking lot pavement. A well-lit lump under that row of lights. Wearing my black funeral hat. Dramatic …

Wonder if Susan will ever marry. She seems happy enough with Grant the way things are. Lord, when I think of how scandalized by that I'd have been years ago! Suppose part of me still is. What do you think, Jackie? Okay, you just go on resting your old orange head on the railing and saying nothing. You're a good listener, I'll say that for you. Yes, Susan's happy. After all, she has that whole office full of girls to manage. To push around. No, that's not fair. Susan's been good to me, in her own way. Weren't for me she'd probably have pulled up stakes and moved to Toronto long ago. She's ambitious, Susan is.

Can't blame her for that. I was ambitious too. Always felt I had to make something out of myself, always a little on the defensive. Maybe I resented the fact Harry had a degree and I didn't. But I did all right for a girl who started out on a dirt-poor farm. Didn't exactly shake the entire teaching profession. But did all right, just the same. Normal school was considered a good education for a girl in my day. Teachers get away with murder today. Lord, when I think of how we had to mind our P's and Q's!

Susan's thirty-eight now. I was expecting Paul when I was her age. Except she's fat and I'm thin, guess we're alike in a lot of ways. Maybe that's why we don't get along. They say that happens when two people are too much alike. Opposites attract; like repels. But that doesn't add up when it comes to Paul. We're not a bit alike yet he's moved as far away from me as it's possible to get. *Why does your son hate you so much, Mrs. Hunter?* Never forget the time one of his friends got drunk and asked me that. But Paul was only eighteen then. He's a grown man now. He has teenagers of his own. He must understand why I wouldn't let him buy that motorcycle. Never can tell what Paul's thinking. A good-looking man, but somehow a totally inexpressive face. *Why does your son hate you?* That question has haunted me for years.

Mea Culpa. No doubt I protected him too much … in too many ways. And all I succeeded in doing was breaking his spirit.

Getting windy out here. Windy and cold. Dark wind brushing my cheeks, tugging at my hair, seems to be pulling me closer and closer against the railing, drawing me with it over the very edge. What was that old soap opera I used to watch? *The Edge of Night.* That was it. That's where I am now. At the edge of night. And life's nothing but a soap opera after all.

Maybe I didn't break Paul's spirit. Maybe he didn't have all that much spirit to begin with. Nice thought, that. If I'm not a ball-breaker, I'm certainly a bitch. I can remember a time when I wouldn't have dared even to think such words. World's changed so much. Either go along with it or …

or what?

or jump …

small loss, after all. One entirely superfluous old white-haired lady with a sore nose and an aching shoulder …

No. I can't do that to Susan. Or Paul. Maybe I've made mistakes, but I've always done the best I could with what I knew at the time. Nobody gets a trial run at parenting. Right, Jackie? Besides there are still things to be enjoyed: winter children to watch at play, spring blossoms to smell, music to listen to, still so much. Better to struggle on with whatever time I have left. But I can't struggle on here. Have to be my own person again. Die in the saddle as it were … in my own kitchen. Better still, in my garden. Anyway, who knows? Could live another ten years. Fear's what I have to kill. Fear and indecision. And tired old ladies with sad eyes and drooping mouths.

Good-bye, Jackie.

Now *that's* littering. One dead pumpkin down below. In a black velvet hat. Forgot about that. Never mind. Never liked that hat anyway. Now to call Susan. She'll be surprised to hear I'm going home. She'll argue like mad. But I am going home. For better or worse, I *am* going home.

Afterword

Norma West Linder's collection *No Common Thread* may appear a random selection of her short fiction, but the stories share a common trait: everyday people searching for meaningful relationships with others, be they family, friends, or strangers. It is this elusive tie that binds us all, like the delicate threads of a patchwork comforter. The over thirty-year span among the stories in this collection illustrates the timelessness of this universal theme.

Through her sharp dialogue and incisive descriptions, Linder reveals many identifiable characters – widows and drifters, artists and immigrants, gigolos and housewives – the varied kinds of people one may meet in a number of chance encounters in one's life. Delving into their unique perspectives, Linder engages in the conversations we often wish we had had with them. She explores the fears and insecurities that stand in the way of personal connections and celebrates the hopes and joys that come with greater human understanding. These stories of happy reunions and tragic estrangements evoke an empathy that compels us to read on.

I have known Norma for several years, having first met her at a Sarnia writers' workshop in 2006. To my delight, I discovered that we share a special connection to Manitoulin Island, where we each grew up, decades apart. Norma has always been supportive of beginning writers, recognizing hidden talent despite our self-doubts, an astute perceptiveness evident in this captivating work of her selected fiction.

Ryan Gibbs
Professor of English
Lambton College

A Note on the Author

Norma West Linder was born in Toronto during 1928, but spent her childhood on Manitoulin Island and her teenage years in Muskoka. She is a member of The Writers' Union of Canada, International PEN, The Ontario Poetry Society, and The Canadian Federation of Poets. She was a founding member of Writers in Transition and served as President of the Sarnia Branch of the Canadian Authors Association.

Linder is the author of five novels, fourteen collections of poetry (a volume of her selected poems was published in 2012), a memoir of Manitoulin Island, a children's book, and a biography of Pauline McGibbon. For twenty-four years she was on the faculty of Lambton College, teaching English and Creative Writing. For seven years she wrote a monthly column for *The Sarnia Observer*. Her short stories have been published internationally, are widely anthologized, and have been broadcast on CBC radio. She lives in Sarnia and is the mother of two adult daughters and a son.

Other Publications by Norma West Linder

NOVELS
    The Lemon Tree
    Tangled Butterflies
    Woman in a Blue Hat
    Nahanni (co-author with Hope Morritt)
    The Savage Blood

POETRY
    On the Side of the Angels
    Ring Around the Sun
    Pyramid
    The Rooming House
    This Age of Reason
    Matter of Life and Death
    Morning Child
    Jazz in the Old Orange Hall
    River of Lethe: A Journey Through Alzheimer's
    Magical Manitoulin
    Days of Draper Township School S.S. #1
    When Angels Weep
    Lovely as a Tree
    Adder's-tongues

BIOGRAPHY
    Pauline: A warm look at Ontario Lt.-Gov. Pauline McGibbon
        (co-author with Hope Morritt)

ONE-ACT PLAY
    Haggerty and the Big One

FOR CHILDREN
    Corey

MEMOIR
    Morels and Maple Syrup

CPSIA information can be obtained at www.ICGtesting.com
Printed in the USA
LVOW13s1907120713

342493LV00002B/12/P

9 781897 475911